AUG 09 2021

W9-CBF-635

The Woman
from Uruguay

The Woman from Uruguay

Pedro Mairal

**Translated by
Jennifer Croft**

BLOOMSBURY PUBLISHING

NEW YORK · LONDON · OXFORD · NEW DELHI · SYDNEY

BLOOMSBURY PUBLISHING
Bloomsbury Publishing Inc.
1385 Broadway, New York, NY 10018, USA

BLOOMSBURY, BLOOMSBURY PUBLISHING, and the Diana logo
are trademarks of Bloomsbury Publishing Plc

First published in the United States 2021

Bloomsbury Publishing Plc does not have any control over, or responsibility
for, any third-party websites referred to or in this book. All internet addresses
given in this book were correct at the time of going to press. The author and
publisher regret any inconvenience caused if addresses have changed or sites
have ceased to exist, but can accept no responsibility for any such changes.

ISBN: HB: 978-1-63557-733-4; EBOOK: 978-1-63557-734-1

LIBRARY OF CONGRESS CATALOGING-IN-PUBLICATION DATA IS AVAILABLE

2020946474

2 4 6 8 10 9 7 5 3 1

Typeset by Westchester Publishing Services
Printed and bound in the U.S.A. by Berryville Graphics Inc.,
Berryville, Virginia

To find out more about our authors and books visit
www.bloomsbury.com and sign up for our newsletters.

Bloomsbury books may be purchased for business or promotional use.
For information on bulk purchases please contact Macmillan Corporate
and Premium Sales Department at specialmarkets@macmillan.com.

ONE

You told me I talked in my sleep. That's the first thing I remember from that morning. The alarm went off at six. Maiko had gotten into bed with us. You nestled into me and the words were whispered in my ear, so as not to wake him, but also I think to keep us from facing each other, from talking with our morning breath.

"Want me to make you some coffee?"

"No, my love. You two keep sleeping."

"You were talking in your sleep. You scared me."

"What did I say?"

"The same thing as last time: 'Guerra.'"

"Weird."

"Very. 'Guerra'? Meaning 'war'?"

I took a shower, got dressed. Gave you and Maiko a Judas kiss.

"Have a good trip," you said.

"See you tonight."

"Be careful."

I took the elevator down to the garage in the basement and drove out. It was still dark. I didn't put on any music. I went down Billinghurst, turned on Libertador. There was already some traffic, mostly semis closer to the port. In the Buquebus parking lot, the attendant informed me they were full. I had to go back out and leave the car in a lot on the other side of the avenue. I didn't like that because it meant that when I came back that night I'd have to walk those two dark blocks along the abandoned train tracks with all my savings on me, in cash.

At the check-in counter there wasn't any line. I handed over my ID.

"Fast ferry to Colonia?" the agent asked me.

"Yes, and the bus to Montevideo."

"Coming back today, as well, on the direct?"

"Yes."

"Right . . ." he said, looking at me just a second too long. He printed my ticket and handed it to me with an icy smile. I avoided his eyes. He made me nervous. Why had he looked at me like that? Could they be making a list of the people who went and came back in one day?

I went up the escalator to go through Customs. I sent my backpack through the scanner, circled through the empty labyrinth of ropes. "Next," they called. The immigration officer checked my ID, my ticket. "Alright, Lucas, stand in front of the camera if you would, please. Excellent. Put your right thumb . . . Thank you."

I took my ticket and my ID and entered the departure lounge. The rest of the passengers were there already, in one long line. Through the glass I could see the ferry completing its maneuvers to dock. I bought the most expensive coffee and croissant in history (a sticky croissant, a radioactive coffee) and devoured them instantly. I went to the end of the line and heard some Brazilian couples around me, some French people, and some accent from elsewhere in Argentina, the North, maybe Salta. There were other men going solo, like me; maybe they were also going to Uruguay for the day, for work or to bring back cash.

The line moved, and I walked down the carpeted hallways and got on the ferry. The biggest section, with all those rows of seats, looked a little like a movie theater. I found a place by the window, sat down and sent you a message: *All aboard. Love you.* I looked out the window. It was getting light now. A yellow mist had swallowed up the jetty.

That's when I wrote the email you later found:
Guerra, I'm on my way. 2pm okay?
I never left my email open. Ever. I was very, very careful about that. It comforted me that there was a part of my brain I didn't share with you. I needed my lock on the door, my privacy, my shadow run, even if only for some quiet. It terrifies me the way couples become conjoined: same opinions, same degree of drunkenness, as if man and wife shared one bloodstream. There must

be a chemical leveling that occurs after years of maintaining that constant choreography. Same place, same routines, same diet, simultaneous sex life, identical stimuli, shared temperature, income, fears, incentives, walks, plans . . . What kind of two-headed monster gets created that way? You get symmetrical with your partner, metabolisms synchronize, you operate as mirror images; a binary being with a single set of desires. And the kids are there to giftwrap that lockstep and slap an eternal bow on it. The idea is pure suffocation.

I say "idea" because I think both of us fought against it despite the fact that we were slowly being conquered by inertia. My body stopped ending at my fingertips; it kept going into yours. A single body. There wasn't any Lucas, any Catalina anymore. But then the hermeticism was punctured, cracked: me talking in my sleep, you reading my emails . . . In some parts of the Caribbean, couples name their kid a composite of their names. If we'd had a daughter, we could have called her Lucalina, for example, and Maiko we could have named Catalucas. That's the name of the monster you and I were, decanting into each other. I don't care for that idea of love. I need a nook of my own. Why did you go through my emails? Were you trying to pick the fight, to tell me how you really felt at last? I never checked your emails. You always left your inbox open, and that decreased my curiosity, true. But it also just wouldn't have occurred to me to start rifling through your things.

The ferry set sail. The dock got smaller. You could see a bit of the coast out the window, guess at the buildings, their outlines. What an enormous relief. To leave. Even if it was just for a little while. To get out of the country. The loudspeakers announced the safety guidelines—in Spanish, in Portuguese, in English. Life vests under every seat. A moment later: "We are pleased to inform you that the duty-free shop is now open." Whoever invented the term "duty-free" is a genius. The more restrictions they put on trade, the more we like that term in Argentina. What a bizarre idea of freedom.

Here I was, traveling to smuggle in my own money. My advance on my last book. The cash that was going to solve everything. Even my depression, my sense of imprisonment, and the great "of course not" overriding everything in my life. Not going out because I don't have any money, not sending the letter, not printing the form, not inquiring with the agency, not letting on how mad I am, not painting the chairs, not handling the mold, not sending out my résumé. And why not? Because I don't have any money.

I'd opened the account in Montevideo in April. Only now, in September, were the advances from Spain and Colombia coming in, despite my having signed the contracts ages ago. If they had transferred the money in dollars to Argentina, the bank would have converted it into pesos at the official rate and then taken off the tax. If I went to pick it up in Uruguay and brought it back in bills, I could exchange it in Buenos Aires at the unofficial exchange rate and end up with over twice as much. The trip was worth it, worth even the risk that they'd catch me with the cash at Customs on the way back, since I was planning to cross the border with more dollars than anyone was allowed to bring into the country.

The River Plate: never has its name—from the Spanish word for "silver," and the South American for "cash"— been more apt. The water was beginning to gleam. I was going to be able to pay you back what I owed you for the months I hadn't had any work, when we'd lived off your salary alone. I was going to be able to dedicate my time exclusively to writing for ten months or so, if I was careful about what I spent. The sun was coming out. My losing streak was coming to an end.

I remember that day we actually paid the toll on the highway in coins. We were going to visit my brother in Pilar. The woman in the booth couldn't believe it. She counted the coins, fifteen pesos in coins. "There's fifty centavos missing," she said. The honking had started behind us. "It has to all be there, count it again," I said. "It's fine, just go," she said, and we took off laughing, you and I, but deep down there was something painful about it, I think, something we never confessed. Because you used to say: we have some issues with our finances, not with how much money we have. And I thought you were right. But I kept not finishing projects, kept not quite finalizing any deals with anyone. I didn't want to teach, and a silence was born and grew bigger with every passing month, as the kitchen sink fell in and I propped it up with some cans, and the Teflon got scratched in our pots, as one of the light fixtures in the living room burned out and left us in partial darkness, as the washing machine broke, and the old oven began to give off a strange smell, and the steering wheel in the car shook like the a space shuttle making its way through the atmosphere . . . And my tooth ended up only half fixed because the crown was expensive, and we suspended your IUD until further notice, we owed two months at Maiko's preschool, we fell behind on our bills, our premiums, and one day both our cards were declined at Walmart while Maiko threw a tantrum on the floor between the registers, and we had to return all the items we had put in our cart. We were angry and ashamed. Insufficient funds.

We fought on the balcony, once, and then again in the kitchen, you sitting on the marble counter, legs crossed, crying, putting ice on your eyes. "I have to go to work tomorrow with my eyes like this, fuck," you were saying. You were fed up with me, with my toxic cloud, my pollution. "You seem beaten," you told me, "defeated. I don't get what you want." I was standing next to the refrigerator, anesthetized, not knowing what to say. I flailed about, I felt cornered and couldn't think of anything better to talk about than my own frustration. I provoked you just to see what you would say. "If you want to limit your sex life to a couple of orgasms a month, you do that, I can't live this way," I told you.

When I went out or finished a reading or spoke on some roundtable at some cultural center, I'd have a drink, and someone would come up and talk to me, a girl of twenty-five or a MILF of fifty, ask me a question, smile at me, want it, want me, and I'd think, just a couple of beers and then off to the telo, the hourly hotel, a little adventure, my fangs would come out, I was a lion tied up with deli string, "I have to go," I'd say, a kiss on the cheek, "Too bad," she'd say, "Yeah, I have a small child, bucket of cold water, he'll wake me up tomorrow." That's it, *c'est fini*.

And I'd go out into the night, get on a bus, get home, you'd be sleeping, I'd spoon you, hold you, nothing, you'd be exhausted, fast asleep. Maiko would come and get in bed with us early. We'd get up. We'd make him his Nesquik, take him to preschool, you'd go to the city center. "Chau, see you tonight," and when you'd come back, you'd be tired and want to go to bed without dinner, and I'd watch TV, accumulating anger, venomous testosterone. We'd go on like that for months.

"Am I supposed to congratulate you for not fucking some girl?" you asked me, "Am I supposed to say thank you?" You were raring for a fight, a big one. And you would not let it go. You're good at arguing. "Tell me what it is you want," you were saying. I didn't say any more. I didn't want to go on.

At what point did the monster you and I were start getting paralyzed? We used to fuck standing up, remember? On the terrace at your apartment on Agüero, up against that wardrobe we painted together, in the shower, on the dining room table one time. We were splendid, wanting one another. Hungry for each other. From the front, lifting up your leg against the wall, from the back on the armchair, knocking over the table arrangements, you on top and arching suddenly like you were about to be abducted by an alien spacecraft. We'd think of things, we'd switch positions, rotating, dynamic, on fire. Gradually our beast with two backs grew hobbled, lay down, didn't get up again, or got up only because the bed was there, because we were touching, horizontal, the beast now lazy, our orgasms derived from just one position, predictable missionary, or maybe you'd be facedown, almost absent. Together and alone. Or those nights when you were so tired you didn't even make it all the way into bed, staying suspended between the quilt and the sheet, and later in the darkness I would get under the sheet and not even be able to spoon you, let alone slip my hand under the waist of your pajamas, or hold your breasts, or kiss your neck, we were separated by the taut fabric, next to each other but inaccessible, as if on two distinct planes of reality.

Most nights it went like that. I lay awake on my back, listening to your breathing—and then, around two in the morning, the drip that we would never identify the source of, the exact sound of insomnia, the leak of the unconscious. The most annoying part was that it flowed irregularly, it was unpredictable; but it was accumulating somewhere, no doubt forming a puddle, creating more mold, rotting the plaster, the cement, weakening the structure of the household. I'd have to go to the armchair in the living room, surf the web a little more, fall asleep there, then go back to bed, defeated. Because I guess you were right, I was defeated, I don't know exactly why or by whom, but I took pleasure in it. "I was down for the count for a long time, a lover of errors," goes the song I'd sing drunk later that day.

I'd defeated myself, I suppose. My mental monologue, my contrarian's stand. When I'm not writing or working, the volume of the words in my head goes way up, and I am inundated. Doubts grew like vines, surrounding me. I wondered who you were seeing. Those late nights when you'd be so dressed up and tired after meetings and drinks with the foundation . . . And those subtle changes: you used to rarely be waxed, and now I could feel how smooth your legs were whenever I brushed against you in bed. My head flooded with questions. Were you prepping and preening for someone who wasn't me? And where were you meeting him, Cata? In telos? You'd never been one for telos, but maybe that was precisely what now made you curious. I wondered who it could be, I had nothing to go on, I figured it might be a member of the board, maybe. The triangle of your pubic area, always so seventies, such a bush, now seemed pruned, reduced, a little sharper. "For my swimsuit," you told me, and it's true you said that in December, with yet another summer of invitations to pools and backyards on its way.

You went to the gynecologist and got your yeast infection treated, and you made me take the same medication in case I had it, too. Were we getting it treated, getting rid of that odor, for him, whoever he was? Those late nights piled up, when you'd come back after dinner, at one, two in the morning, and from our bed I would hear you in the bathroom letting the water run a long time, lots of soaping, taking off your makeup, using the bidet, brushing your teeth. I'm almost certain you started smoking again, and who with? I could almost see you on terraces with a glass of champagne in your hand and a cigarette, your smoking style, your smile. All of that washed away on your pit stop in the bathroom. One time you actually showered before getting into bed. Another night I smelled cologne on you, strong, though I'll admit I am sensitive when it comes to smells, hypersensitive, and it might have been that it was just from all the kisses goodbye at your big end-of-year dinner. Where was your heart among all those cardiologists? You withdrew more and more, hiding inside yourself and rooting around in me trying to find something. Whenever my jealousy would ruffle me I'd get the urge to email you a set of instructions on how to be successful as a secret lover: you don't just have to be waxed and careful, you also have to keep a clean pair of panties in your purse, use the bidet before and after every fuck, keep your obsession in check, postpone dates when you have your period, block his cell. Successful secret lovers don't get periods. They don't call, they don't give gifts. They don't bite in bed or wear blush or perfume. They leave no traces on the surface of the body. They simply sizzle with pleasure. They activate the central nervous system, turn it on from within.

I was so naive. I had no idea about anything, embracing my role as the cast-off old man. Fortunately I never emailed you. I ruminated, chewed on my insecurities. That was my unemployed position, the stance of a man who can't provide. That was my impotence, asking you if you could transfer me some money, semicovertly requesting ten thousand pesos from my brother while he barbecued, and those Excel spreadsheets you loved to make so much, my numbers in red, my debt increasing. None of it was particularly erotic, I'll admit. And it's true that Mr. Lucas was now slightly older, slightly less attractive. Or at least that's how I felt. My back was giving out on me, the roll of fat on my skinny-guy's belly getting more prominent, stray grays on my head and my crotch, and then there was my dick that from one day to the next seemed to lean slightly to the right, like my compass had gone crazy and abandoned the north to point a little to the east, toward Uruguay. That's what it was more than anything: my mind was elsewhere. And sometimes when you came back early, you'd find me watching the sunset on the balcony, clinging like a prisoner to the rail we'd put in when Maiko took his first few steps.

The vibration of the ship had put me to sleep. When I opened my eyes again, the sun had come out over the river. We were coming up on Colonia already. My phone got reception again, and there was Guerra's email answering mine:

Great. 2pm. Same place as last time. Then I said her name, to myself, up against the glass, looking out at the water that gleamed like liquid silver.

"Magalí Guerra Zabala."

I repeated it twice.

TWO

They announced over the loudspeakers that we were about to arrive, informed those passengers who were traveling with their cars that they could now go down into the hold, but that they were "to not turn on their engines until instructed." Splitting the infinitive. I went up close to the exit, one of the first, wanting to get a good seat on the bus. But there was an immediate agglomeration of people. Those moments when you feel like cattle at the slaughterhouse. Everyone watching the closed door. We were on the verge of mooing. Then it opened.

I'm in Uruguay, I thought, walking down that tin sleeve with see-through nylon windows. I went through Customs almost on tiptoe and went out to where the buses were. There was a guy ahead of me who stopped to smoke a cigarette, so I got there first. Or that's what I thought. When I got on, I realized the bus was full of people. Maybe they were from another ferry.

"Montevideo?"

"Yep," said the chauffeur.

"Should I wait for the next one?" I asked in the hope they would have me board an emptier, roomier bus.

"No, no. There's room in the back."

I got on again, resigned. Those faces. I didn't see a single empty seat. Then in the back I saw one, just where I wanted: by the window on the right side. I said excuse me; the man sitting in the aisle got up and let me by. When I sat down I realized why it was empty: it was the seat where the back wheel takes up most of the space for your feet. I was going to have an uncomfortable ride, but I'd be looking out at the highway in the direction I preferred; even if you couldn't see it, you could still sense on that side of the landscape the nearness of the sea.

The bus started up, left the port, and got on the highway lined with palms. What was it about those gigantic trees that delighted me so much, flashing by, inexhaustible, repeated, like a portal to another place, transit to the tropics, an African spark? What combination of things triggered that attack of happiness? The whiter light, the bus that wobbled, the crossing of large swathes, the friendly, broken, undulating landscape, so far from the fucking metaphysical pampa of Argentina, the morning, a pony grazing, giving in to that state of non-being you get into when you travel, the clouds . . . Over the window it said "Emergency Exit," just those words against the backdrop of the sky. It seemed like a metaphor for something. The possibility of escape into the blue.

It wasn't exactly the sea you could divine behind those undulating fields, it was still the river, the end of the estuary that went on to be the sea, but you could sense it like something that was just about to happen, a glint in my mind where Guerra was, too, in that other brightness among the dunes the summer I met her in Rocha. It was on that horizon that the whole memory took place, and it was closer and closer now.

I met her at the festival in Valizas, where I'd been invited to read. It went from Friday to Monday, the last weekend of January. You had stayed back with Maiko at your sister's place in the suburbs. The trip was fun because there were other writers there. The whole place was fairly hippie-ish, with bunkbeds in the rooms and shared bathrooms. The schedule of readings and roundtables was just an excuse to meet people, to walk around between the dunes, to smoke, to hear people's opinions, their ludicrous theories, to laugh, to swim in the ocean, to get caught up with the latest gossip from the literary world. The readings were good, but I was more interested in the periphery. Meeting Gustavo Espinosa, for example, drinking yerba mate with him, discussing his book *Las arañas de Marte* . . .

We wandered. The place was full of rich kids playing paupers for a month. Shabby blondes, Rastafarians at expensive universities, temporary artisans, half-time musicians, full-time jugglers. The place had its charms, and you could walk around it hearing people playing the guitar, singing "Let's step up the hope, muchachos" or that Radiohead one where they say "You're so fucking special." And there were yerba mate sessions, cannabis circles, groups playing drums. Some people did all that at once. Lots of scraggly beards, braids, hair that was salty from some weeks-long impasse with shampoo, girls with long hair and primordial attitudes and surprising green eyes, dressed in a mix of gym sweatshirts and ethnic fabrics, a Bali vibe, a Bombay vibe, Buddhist allusions, overacted Africanisms, tents scattered in the sand, camps, the pinnacle of homeless chic. Marijuana made me feel like I belonged there. A fortysomething hanging around with kids in their twenties.

I wasn't the only one there who was elderly and eclipsed. There was Norberto Vega, there was Marcelo Luján . . . I hung out with those two the most. Vega was amazed by the hygienic conditions—or the lack thereof. When I went to take a shower in the shared bathroom, he warned me: "Don't you shower here, Luquitas, the smallest fungus on these hippies is the size of a Smurf house!" I showered anyway. And Marcelo had this smile I hadn't seen on him for a while: constant, in a state of grace. It was the drugs, of course, but also the fact that he was absorbed in a world without obligations, without any need for responsibility of any kind, no family, no work, no schedule, no city, no cars, no danger of accidents, just soft sand everywhere, heat. Beach hedonism, pure and simple. When we suddenly couldn't take it anymore, we'd go to the bunk beds to nap for a few hours in the middle of the day, covered in sand, just to hide from the yowl of the sun.

Then I had to get into the sea to clear my head and be alert for my roundtable. The cold saltwater revived me. At first when I spoke into the microphone I think I was fine, somewhat on autopilot, but eventually I started really saying something. Vega was slumping down in his chair, yawning like a lion at the zoo. Marcelo, while others were speaking, wore the expression of someone possessed and remote-controlled, or someone who'd just been informed by text message that he was adopted. Still, I think we did a good job, we held on to our dignity, we were slightly polemical and maybe even slightly funny. It was in a big barbecue area with a table, audio equipment, chairs for the audience and behind them a number of tables for an expo of independent publishers. It was a friendly atmosphere, and it was full, with people leaning out the windows. We talked about realism, verisimilitude, new technologies, the nineties, post-dictatorship Argentina . . . There we were, Latin American intellectuals putting on our dog and pony show, talking to ourselves at a beach resort. People were looking at us, I don't know how much we were getting across, I felt like they wanted us to read something, more story, less theory, although they all applauded enthusiastically. After that there was a party, and that's where Guerra came in.

Now the bus was passing through some yellow fields that were almost phosphorescent on account of the flowers of something I don't know the name of. The palm trees were behind us now. You could see off in the distance little farms and eucalyptus clusters. Every now and then, right by the highway, there would be a house with a neatly kept and decorated lawn. One with a cement horse, plaster swans, and antique carts. Another with the bodies of trucks from the fifties. That quasi-Cuban element you see in rural Uruguay, with the old Chevys and stripped Lanchesters, some that still work, others that remain makeshift chicken coops until some fanatic restorer comes along.

I wanted to get out into the aisle to stretch my legs, but for that I'd have needed to say excuse me to my seat-mate and I preferred to hold out a little longer. Toward the middle of the bus, across the way, a guy answered his cell phone and started screeching into it. He was explaining something to his secretary, coordinating shifts: he was a doctor. He was imposing his bellowing on the sleep and daydreams of all the other passengers, his scheduling issues, his abuse of that woman who was just trying to put his messy commitments in order. "You can put off the Medical Group thing until October! For the love of God, Isabel, don't plug everything into the same week, give it just a tiny bit of thought!"

I've never liked male doctors, with their air of over-grown children in overalls, chronic gigantic schoolkids, the bald show-offs in the class, pretending to be serious in the office, using big anatomical words, oversexed, libidinous the second they shut their office door, all of them fucking their nurses in the staff-only back of the ER, restricted access, authorized personnel, hospital-bed sex, debauchery in some unlit corner, between the oxygen and the carts of surgical equipment. Overalls hiding erections, physicians with priapism, huge knowledgeable cocks, revered cocks, Hippocratic phalluses surrounded by pussies as available as pink little butterflies in the air, satyrs in white, with a few gray hairs that make the female patient sigh, "And now take a deep breath for me, now another, good, raise your shirt a little, deep breath, good . . ." Sons of bitches, rapid-fire predators, insurance butchers, accumulating commissions on unnecessary C-sections, postponing the operation until after their little jaunt to Punta del Este, serial abusers, time thieves, health thieves, I hope they get a hell that's a waiting room that has magazines with their pages all stuck together, those exploiters posing in their Greek colonnade, just apply the ointment to the pruriginous area, you son of a truck filled with bitches! "The pruriginous area," why wouldn't you just say "the place where it itches," you sisterfucking grandiloquent piece of shit . . .

Luquitas, you used to want to be a doctor, you just quit on the way to becoming one, whispered the opposing council, the Greek chorus that always traveled with me, *you dropped out in your first year, remember?* Yeah, so? What does that have to do with anything! *And now a doctor is fucking your wife. What an irony. The great scriptwriter has done it again. What a fantastic goal they scored on you, man. Curling it right into the corner. You're the goalie in the air hearing the ball bounce off the net. It hurts, it hurts, but it, too, will pass.*

I'm going to give you a prescription for a topical you'll apply to the clobberwhipped area, to your EndoBag, and that lomlopiratic irritation, it's really terrific, it'll reduce your cranial cornea, cure your chronic hinditis, release your cuckoldean knot . . . You'll see. You're going to be just fine. Just take a deep breath if you would, lower your pants a little more . . . There you go, and it didn't hurt at all, now did it?

And just that morning I'd looked at your earrings in the bathroom, dangly, silver, expensive, discarded as soon as you got home and took off your makeup, the mascara I never saw, and I remembered that Caribbean expression: she's off swinging her earrings with just anybody. Who were you swinging your earrings with, Catalina? Your Ricciardi earrings swaying from that sexual gallop, your Quintana Avenue jewelry jangling in the frisson of your affair, sounding like the crystals of a chandelier in the middle of an earthquake. The director of development of the Cardio Life Foundation grinding her pelvic pelt on the member of a member of the executive board of the same. Some stuck-up little doctor, nice car, a Catholic, mass in the burbs, an ex-rugby-player cardiologist, thick neck, baptism certificates of every kid in his wallet, English-style office, a green lamp with a bronze horse, boiserie, kind of dark in the waiting room, fox-hunting prints, a horse leaping over a fence, a rowdy pack of hounds, burgundy wallpaper, an older secretary, approved by the wife, trying to cover and coordinate his unexpected obligations.

Finally the guy shut up.

I'll admit that I was anxious, that my nerves were fried, that I was agitated, urging onward. Now you really could see, past the fields, a blue horizon. We were about to cross the bridge that went over the Santa Lucía River. The sea! The landscape opened up, some ravines, the land ended for a second, and the water appeared, the coast of the Atlantic, she was already there, on my fingertips, in the air in front of my face, her haughty face, the challenge in her eyes as she squinted slightly, serious and then with a half-smile in the corners of her lips, mischievous, fierce, everything at once, how she looked at me when I saw her in Valizas for the first time and asked her to dance. There was a jukebox where the barbecue was, and they were playing cumbias and salsas, and somebody put on "Overdose of Love, Overdose of Passion."

I had already been dancing in the tumult, a little tease with the Chilean poet, but she was dancing more for Vega than for me, and there was Guerra to one side with a friend, chatting, a glass of beer in her hand, and I took her by the other hand and brought her to the dance floor, she'd wanted to, she'd already seen me, she told me later, she'd heard me speak, she smiled, she held my gaze, she twirled around and looked at me again, our eyes locked, and I felt the strength she had, the strength in her hands, skinny with a terrestrial energy, nothing flighty about her, dancing to the fullest, when I took her by the hands and twirled her, or when I spun her like a top till she was wrapped up in my arm, a girl who packed heat, ready for battle, Bettie bangs, wet hair, denim miniskirt, T-shirt loose over her bikini bra (her "soutien," she would have said), and barefoot. Barefoot all summer long. What a gorgeous girl, and what a fire demon exploded inside me and rampaged through my blood. "What's your name?" "Magalí." "I'm Lucas." We went to get more beer.

There was a kiosk that sold drinks off to one side. I don't really remember what we talked about. I know I got all puffed up like a cobra in front of her, with questions born of genuine curiosity, so many questions. I made her laugh. She talked to me. We danced more. We drank more. She hadn't read my books or taken notice of my name. She was there because her friend ran a poetry press. She told me she had started on a degree in social science, dropped out, and that she was now working for a newspaper in the afternoons in Montevideo, that she was in Valizas for two weeks—with some friends, she said, a little evasive on that subject. The next beer we had to venture farther for, to a store down the street, a dark stretch, and on the way there I took her by the hand, and she put her arm around my waist, and I gave her a kiss, we gave each other a kiss. A long one. I was dead, and I resurrected myself. I was blind, and I could see again at last. I was anesthetized, and all five senses came back in full force. "I have to be careful," she said into my ear. "Why? Do you have a boyfriend?" "Something like that," she whispered. "I'm married, I have a kid." "I know, you mentioned your kid at your talk."

I loaned her my sweater, because she was cold. I told her where I'd been that day, on the beach, to one side of a stream, and that I had seen a line of people on the other side, climbing a dune. "They were going to Polonio," she said. "You can get to Cabo Polonio from here?" "Yeah, it's a couple of hours on foot." "Want to go tomorrow?" I challenged her. She hesitated, calculated incalculable things in her head, got serious, said: "Yeah, tomorrow I'll show you, we'll need to go early."

We went back to the party, and there was her friend, she took her hand, said she had to help her with some boxes of books. We said goodbye demurely, a kiss on the cheek, saying nothing of our date the next day. The music was still going, but no one was dancing anymore. I stayed, stood there alone with a glass in my hand, trying to take in the shock and thinking of how she'd told me she didn't have a cell phone, how I had no way of contacting her. One of the organizers saw me and said, almost yelling over the music: "We canceled the table tomorrow at eleven, so you're free." When two people are attracted to each other, a strange telekinesis opens up a path between them that removes all obstacles. It's that clichéd. Mountains are moved aside. It was three in the morning, and I went to sleep drunk on all of that, without an ounce of guilt.

The rural emptiness of the road grew populated bit by bit. There were sheds with equipment for sale, a few factories, rows of low houses, schools. I started listening to an exchange in the seats just behind me. A woman was answering a question that I didn't quite catch but could guess: the man wanted to know the reason she was traveling to Montevideo. Her mother had passed away after a long illness. That is always painful, he was saying, the death of a loved one, and he said that each of us has our own way of mourning. "If you're a believer, you can assimilate it better." "Of course," she said, "you can keep up the hope that one day you'll see them again."

I got caught up in that exchange that, as often happens in casual conversations between strangers, immediately turned transcendental. The beyond, being reunited with family members, resurrection, the immortality of souls, the mystery. "What is your religion?" asked the man. "Jehovah's Witness," answered the woman. "Ah," he said, "I belong to the Evangelical Church, where I'm a pastor." All the empathy that had arisen now evaporated, their voices getting hesitant and tense. Gently he attacked her dogma, provoked her on the point of the Holy Spirit, then miracles, he quoted from memory Acts 13. I couldn't free myself now. I wanted to see where this tender confrontation would end, their divergences on the apocalypse, their battle of Christian apostates. She argued her side pretty well. The pastor kept saying "you people" when speaking to the woman. "You people have this attitude toward miracles that . . . well . . . because miracles exist. A lot of people in my church have been cured through prayer. I have seen people be cured of their flat feet. My grandson himself got rid of his flat foot through prayer. And this one woman's legs had evened out, she'd had one that was shorter before."

The conversation entranced me, the idea of a woman whose legs evened out. What if they'd evened out the wrong way, and the longer leg had retracted and gotten even with the shorter one, and she'd ended up shorter, and now she goes and lodges a complaint with the pastor because she lost something like four inches on her height, and she isn't okay with that miracle, she and her mother come in to complain, "My girl was tall, sure, she had a limp, fine, but she was tall, and now she's squat," and the case winds up in a Brazilian court of the Universal Church of the Kingdom of God.

Then the pastor started talking about forgiveness. I wanted to see their faces. But I couldn't work up the courage to turn around. He told her about how an older lady had come in for a wedding at his church with these stiff legs she could hardly move. There was a three-layer cake, they'd all pitched in to pay for it, which, for those people, was a pretty big deal. The stiff-legged lady wanted to talk to him in private, and they prayed together, her

MIDDLETON
PUBLIC LIBRARY

Checkout Receipt

11/7/2022 12:16:41 PM

Checked Out

Title: The woman from Uruguay /
Due Date: 2022-12-05

Checked Out - Security Still Enabled

Title: Woman's day (magazine)
Due Date: 2022-11-21

Total Checked Out This Session: 2

Thank you for visiting the library!

and the pastor, they said the Lord's Prayer, slowly, and when they got to the part that says "and forgive us our debts, as we also have forgiven our debtors," he repeated the sentence twice, and the lady burst into tears and said she couldn't forgive her son, and then she did forgive him, and she could move her legs again. Everybody at the ceremony was stunned. The pastor reached out to the family some time later, and the woman had died, but at that wedding, she'd been able to walk.

He listed some more examples of people who, as soon as they forgave, improved their situation: kids got jobs, a son-in-law won a brand-new car, just about everything got unblocked. "Even I," said the pastor, "took an awfully long time to forgive my wife. She'd come home late, she worked very unpredictable hours, she'd come back at eleven o'clock at night." He went crazy with jealousy. The devil made him assume the worst. Every couple of hours he'd go crazy thinking about it, and he would pray, and it would pass. He called the devil "the enemy." And in the end he forgave her, without really knowing if she was cheating on him or not, but he forgave her and was free. It used to be that she'd come home and he'd be mean to her, order her to get to cooking. Now he'd have dinner waiting for her with some white chocolate for dessert, because white chocolate was her favorite. They'd been together for thirty-five years.

Who is responsible for this? I thought. Who's put me here in front of these two nutcases who say things that cut straight to the heart of my own crisis? Does everyone pay attention only to the things that apply directly to their own lives, taking from the infinite daily chaos just the snippets that specifically have to do with their situation? Or do such serendipitous things sometimes happen? Was I supposed to forgive you, Catalina? Was that going to liberate and unblock me? Here I was, laughing to myself about the Evangelist and the Jehovah's Witness when, without intending to, without even noticing me, they suddenly schooled me, made me really reflect as I observed the outskirts of Montevideo sliding by. The ramshackle houses, some trash dumps, the hustle, the carts carrying bottles, people sitting talking in the doorways of their shacks, the hill in the distance.

Or was it myself I had to forgive? But forgive for what? I hadn't done anything. Yes, I went with Guerra to Cabo Polonio, but I'm not sure that what happened between us would count as infidelity. Maybe—I don't know. The morning after the party, we met at nine thirty at the old store, our appointed meeting place. I saw her coming in a sarong, a light blue bikini, sneakers. "I didn't think you'd be here," she said. I didn't say it, but I had thought the same thing about her. She was even prettier by day. Wasn't she a little bit out of my league? If I had a shot, I figured it would depend on sucking in my gut and trusting in my dubious aura as an Argentine writer. It might not work.

We didn't kiss at first. We walked side by side, avoiding groups of people sleeping around extinguished campfires.

She was wearing a good pair of sunglasses. I hadn't quite figured her out yet: rude snob or lumpenproletariat? Was she acting like a thug or was she one? I didn't really know Montevideo's sociolects, I couldn't distinguish the nuances. We walked, with long stretches of not talking, smiling at each other every now and then. I didn't want to rush a kiss. I liked that sort of new beginning, sober and in the light of day. We reached a stream. We could either swim across or go by rowboat for a couple of pesos. We decided to swim across because we were committed to having an adventure. We put my backpack and her bag inside a plastic sack that we tied shut. Guerra warned me that we should cross a little bit upstream because the current could drag us out, toward the sea.

It wasn't hard, but she was right that the current was strong, we had to really swim, and we reached the other side almost at the farthest corner of the mouth of the stream. We sat panting on the shore. I took longer to catch my breath than she did.

"You're not going to die on me, are you?" she joked.

"I think I might," I said and threw myself on top of her.

Both of us soaked, like in a romantic movie. But just before I could give her a kiss, she whispered into my ear:

"Let's go farther."

There are two or three Guerra's phrases that continued to echo in my mind for months and made it through the winter without fading. That was one. Let's go farther.

When you're writing, I think, it's hard to convince the reader that a person is attractive. You can say that a woman is beautiful, that a man is good-looking, but where is that dazzling spark, that incandescence in the narrator's gaze, in the obsession? How to show in words the exact configuration of features on a face that bring about an insanity that is maintained over time? And what about her attitude? Her gaze?

I can only say she had an Uruguayan nose. I don't know how to explain it any better than that. Those noses from the East, carried well, that slight warp, the high bridge like the Rs in her name, the insurrectionist defiance of her Basque heritage, in her nose. Not one degree more or one degree less in the angle—that was the mathematical secret of her beauty. And those gigantic green eyes, that mouth that was always positioned for a kiss? Yes, they amplified the sexy, but without the elevation of her battle-ready snout, Guerra wouldn't have been Guerra.

We went up a dune, the first of many, and then down the other side burying our feet in the sand up to our calves. Two hours of this? I thought, but I kept my mouth shut. I wasn't sure I'd be able to make it. Another dune, and from the summit of that one we watched the sea crash, the gleam of atomic explosion. Now I did kiss her. I put my arms around her waist and pressed her to me. A kiss with tongue, an ensnaring kiss, a kiss of perfect intimacy, as though the enormous dome of the sky were coming so close it created our own run of silence. Heat and desire. My hand slow over her hips, flush against her stomach, her bronzed skin and the edge of the thong of her bikini, already at the point of no return, a little farther, she was waxed, and suddenly with the tip of my finger I touched something that wasn't human. Metallic. A tiny extraterrestrial point. A piercing. I looked in her eyes and saw she was amused by my bewilderment. Then my finger vanished into her wet hot pussy, her gorgeous pussy that was wet for me, a wetness that stayed with me as a physical memory that, despite everything that happened, I can locate whenever I want, and that continues to immediately whip up in me a kind of solar revolution that sweeps through the whole network of my arteries and veins.

Guerra was panting, gently biting my mouth as I touched her, and she said:

"Fuck, I want you to fuck me."

Another phrase that made it through the icy winter without losing its heat.

And there was a shriek, or a whistle: people were coming. More pilgrims on the way to Cabo. They were far away, but they still interrupted, and the sky opened back up like a blue eye we couldn't escape. We held each other trying to calm down. It made us laugh, made us euphoric. We kept going. I took out the croissants I'd bought around the corner from the hostel. They were glorious. We devoured them. The sun was intense. We tied our T-shirts around our heads like Bedouins. We had to cross a green valley, and every time we took a break to hold each other, lying in the grass, people would come, pass close by, shouting, and we would have to sit up, pretend, get up and go on. That pedestrian file looked like an exodus, spaced out but there, a nuisance, witnesses, ruiners of intimacy, tramplers of Eden, noisy contingents. I hated all of them and each and every one of them, with their ostentatious faux poverty, their studied display of summer squalor, their high-school-graduation-trip tone, backpacking through Bariloche. And I heard accents from all over, compatriots from Córdoba, Corrientes, Buenos Aires, lots who hadn't gone to Brazil that year because the exchange rate made it too expensive.

Close to Cabo Polonio we hid between the rocks. We were frenzied. Prehistoric rock formations. Nooks, crannies, crevices, slots. That was what we needed.

"I don't have a condom," I told Guerra in haste.

"I do," she said and took some silvery little packets out of her bag.

Guerra undid my swimsuit looking me in the eyes, grabbed me, pulled me toward her, said:

"What a beautiful cock."

Perhaps I am a simple creature, but I'm almost certain that there is nothing in the world a man likes more than being told that. It's better than being told he's a genius, or that you love him, or whatever. And it's such a basic and effective phrase, so easy to lie through. I put on the condom and when I was finally about to put it in we heard a shrill voice:

"Hey, quick question, are we almost to Cabo Polonio?"

A woman's head peeked around the big rock. She didn't realize. From that angle she could only see us from the waist up. Guerra deftly, without any abrupt movements, bent one leg against the rock and closed up her sarong. I pulled my swimsuit back up. I fastened its Velcro. I wished death upon that lost woman then. If I had psychic powers I would have slain her, spontaneous combustion. Now a number of children, all very curious, came springing up out of the rocks.

"You have to keep going a while, and you'll get to the lighthouse," said Guerra.

We were surrounded, laughter, voices, kids hopping from rock to rock.

We kept going, both in a bad mood now, no longer finding it funny. The more people there were around us, the more we cast each other frustrated glances, making serious, complicit, desperate faces. We made it to Cabo, meandered among the picturesque houses, ranches, shacks, got in the ocean to cool our desire, drank beer, and shared a basket of fried fish at a beachside stand. We were silent, and we were calming down. If we couldn't, we couldn't. We mulled over upcoming itineraries: I was going back that evening, and she had to get back, too. The sadness of fresh, just-discovered love. Great confluence of emotions.

I remember that, and I remember that there in Polonio I called her Guerra for the first time:

"Guerra, I'll get hold of you soon enough."

She held my gaze. We talked. I learned a few more things about her. She was twenty-eight. Guerra was the last name of her father, with whom she lived sometimes, and Zabala was the last name of her mother, who'd passed away a few years before. Her boyfriend was a roadie for a metal band that was famous in Uruguay, though I hadn't heard of them. I told her a few things, too. She asked about my books. I told her I was going to send her a novel that took place in Brazil, but that first I had to write it.

We went back in a truck that drove over the sand, then a bus took us back to Valizas. She fell asleep on my shoulder. At some point something started itching, making me uncomfortable, and I realized it was the condom that was still on the tip of my scorched prick.

WE WERE COMING close to the bus station now. My very bent legs and my back were hurting quite a bit. My seatmate was asleep. The pastor and the Jehovah's Witness weren't talking anymore. I realized I was hungry. It was noon. Artigas Boulevard was under construction, and we moved down it slowly, with detours into the opposite lane. Since some people had gotten off at Plaza Cuba, I switched seats. I tried to go over my seatmate, but I woke him up without meaning to. I said I was sorry and sat down closer to the front.

With the seat next to mine empty, it was easier for me to re-create the ghost of Guerra by my side in the bus getting into Valizas. I remember that she woke up because I was shivering, a mix of sunstroke and arousal. I told her everything was going to be okay. She said her stop was a little before mine. She wrote down her email on a slip of paper, and then we said goodbye.

She got off at the entrance to a campsite, and I saw her greet a group of people, one guy with some gray in his hair and a dog in a muzzle who gave her a more extended hug. I reached Valizas just in time to gather my things and get in the writers' minibus that would take us back. I didn't want to talk to anyone. I didn't want to answer any questions about where I'd been or hear about whatever had happened that day. In the random lottery of the seats, I wound up next to a literary critic whose name I'd rather not remember. I curled up next to the window as much as I could, I wanted to dissolve into the setting-sun landscape, give myself over entirely to that sadness of not seeing Guerra again, maybe not for a long time. Suddenly the literary critic brought me back with a question, which went like this, word for word: "Lucas, have you had the opportunity to read what I wrote about the civilization and barbarism axis in your oeuvre?" I answered what I could and afterward, on the four-hour journey to Montevideo, I slept and pretended I was sleeping.

THREE

We arrived at Tres Cruces station. I took my time getting off the bus. I let others go first. The Jehovah's Witness was a wide woman, with silvery hair, in tight jeans, around thirty-five years old, and the pastor, tall and gray, with light-colored eyes, carrying nothing other than a document wallet in his hand, must have been in his sixties. They both looked serious as they got off the bus, and they didn't exchange a word.

I left the bus and went to buy a sandwich. I like how Tres Cruces is kind of a mix between a bus station and a mall, with all sorts of stores on the second floor. I went up the escalator, and I remember immediately sensing the presence of difference. That drift between familiarity and strangeness. A recognizable air, similar to Argentina, in the people, in their speech, the way they dressed, but then suddenly some brands I didn't know, a different word, a "tú" for "you" instead of a "vos," a young couple and the guy with a thermos tucked under his arm and the mate in his hand, walking around with it outside instead of having it at home like we did, a beautiful girl with a little African in her features, and then another, and then another, a premonition of Brazil. Like in dreams, all things in Montevideo strike me as similar but different. They are and they aren't.

I still had some Uruguayan pesos from my previous trip, and an Antel phone card. I ate my sandwich and from a public phone inside the station, I called Enzo. It was like entering the past. I don't know by what bizarre arrangement Enzo wasn't able to receive calls from cell phones. You had to call his landline from a landline, and the strangest part was that he always answered. I had told him I was going to Montevideo, but I surprised him all the same.

"The Dutch!" he said excitedly on the other end of the line.

That's what Enzo calls me, because he says I have a Dutch face, who knows, I don't have even a drop of Dutch blood, but that's been his nickname for me ever since I started going to the writing workshop he gave in Buenos Aires in the nineties.

"Dutch, I'm on the verge of becoming a retiree—a nincompoop! You'd better get here quick before I forget how to get a sentence out."

We agreed to meet at his place at six. That way we'd have a while to talk before my return ferry at nine that night. Enzo always had some book in the works, or just out, he was always just about to go to Paraná, discovering some insane poet, following his curiosity, concocting Uruguay–Buenos Aires–Entre Ríos triangles, arts sections, prologues, readings, prizes, festivals. He was trying to talk me into helping him put together a lit mag that was going to be called *N.o 2* because, according to him, it was only going to last two issues.

I walked in between the counters of the different bus lines with names like Rutas del Plata, Rutas del Sol. I looked at the signs with their destinations: Castillos, La Pedrera, La Paloma, Valizas, and others farther away, Porto Alegre, Florianópolis. How many hours would it take to reach those beaches in the heat of Brazil, the turquoise sea, the caipirinhas? I approached the counter.

"Good morning . . ."

"It's good afternoon, now," said the girl, looking at her watch.

"Good afternoon. I just wanted to know how long the bus to Florianópolis would take."

"It departs at nine at night and arrives at approximately three in the afternoon. Just one person traveling?"

"Yeah, but I don't . . . I was just asking out of curiosity. How much does it cost?"

"One way?"

"Yeah . . ."

"Three thousand five hundred pesos."

"Thank you."

"At your disposal."

I went out of the terminal. I stood waiting for the light to change. The business day, with all its commercial activity, wiped out my Brazilian fantasy. The banks were about to reopen. I went across a little square with restaurants and artisans and the smell of pot in it, and then walked down a diagonal street until I reached 18 de Julio Avenue. My scant orientation in Montevideo depended on that avenue. If I followed it all the way down, I would reach Ciudad Vieja, it was like the central marrow of a peninsula, it ended up having coasts on both sides. And I could mentally place Parque Rodó off in the distance to my left, Cordón over there, Enzo's house to the right farther up in Fernández Crespo, the four plazas, the Plaza de los 33, Cagancha, Entrevero, Independencia, the city center, the area where the banks were, La Pasiva, the music stores, the pedestrian area. That was about it. That was my mental and emotional map, because as soon as I turned, having reached the avenue, I detected that presence of an imagined Montevideo, assembled from my few recollections and the videos Guerra would send me every once in a while. Every couple of weeks she'd send me something over email, so as not to lose me, like Hansel and Gretel's bread crumbs, a song, a *Tremble, Ye Tyrants* clip, a few blocks of her city filmed by anybody with a pulse but that left me intuiting life on the other side. Now, for example, I turned onto the avenue and felt like any of those doors could belong to the bar where Cabrera and Rada sing "I

Held You in the Night." I must have seen the video on YouTube five hundred times, and I'd been humming the song at home, and meanwhile you had absolutely no idea I was burning up on the inside. The camera goes into an empty bar and there are two guys singing that song, one plays the guitar in the most minimal way possible, a string every now and then that accompanies the voices that blend together, "I held you in the night, I was holding you goodbye, you were going out of my life." Guerra would send me those things, and I would be broken, hanging on to that emotion that didn't dissipate. That was Montevideo to me. I was in love with a woman and in love with the city where she lived. And I made up everything about it, or almost everything. An imaginary city in an adjacent country. That was where I walked, more than down real streets.

It wasn't cold. The display windows were already showing off summer wardrobes. A new flashy wave of color in the shopping arcades like textile markets. One little business after the next. In this first stretch everything was toned down, smaller, as if neoliberalism had never happened, no capitalist glamor, old awnings, charmless displays that fascinated me. There was that pastry shop I found so unnerving. I looked at the plaster-like cakes, the petrified meringues, as if they were orders from the eighties that still hadn't been picked up, I found it incredible that they could actually be eaten, a soccer-field cake that looked like it was made out of reinforced concrete. Wouldn't children die after consuming such a thing? Wouldn't they choke on the stucco and glue? The marzipan and that kind of malleable ceramic, the rococo decorations, the flowers made of hard sugar, the frosted blue surfaces, kind of gray, the pearls, the legal coloring . . . all of it supposedly suitable for human consumption.

Maiko's birthday was coming up soon. My train cake had been a hit the previous year among the kids he went to preschool with. All the moms asked how I'd done it. Three pound cakes, chocolate topping, sprinkles, and cubanitos. It was easy. "Genius," they said. When I thought of his cake for this year I got a lump in my throat. His party. It was coming up. In a toy store I saw a dinosaur as tall as a person, thought Maiko would know if it was a velociraptor or what. My kid. That drunken rug rat. Because it was like that at times, like taking care of a plastered dwarf who gets really emotional, cries, and you can't understand what he's saying, you have to keep cutting him off at the pass, you have to carry him because he won't walk, he makes a huge mess at the restaurant, throws things, shouts, falls asleep wherever, you take him home and try to clean him up, and he falls down, gets a bump on his head, shoves around the furniture, falls asleep, throws up at four in the morning.

You know I adore my child. I love him more than anybody in the world. But sometimes he exhausts me, not so much him as my constant worrying about him. Sometimes I think I shouldn't have had a kid at my age.

It's a terrible thing to think, but it has filled my life with a fear that I never had before, fear that something will happen to me and he'll be left an orphan, that something will happen to him, to you. It's a new fragility, a vulnerable side I didn't know I had. Maybe younger parents don't get that. It terrorizes me at times. When he runs all the way to the corner and I can't catch up with him and I scream at him not knowing if he's going to stop. There ought to be a class on raising children. All those prenatal courses and then it's born and when you get back to your house you don't even know where to put it. Where do you set him down, in what part of the house does that tiny little elderly man, that haiku of a person, go? Nobody teaches you that. Nobody warns you how hard it is not to sleep, to give up on yourself all the time, to postpone yourself. Because you will never go back to sleeping eight hours in a row, your permanent soundtrack ends up being "The Sweet Potato Queen," if you want to fuck you have to plan a weekend without the kids a month in advance, you only go to the theater to see movies where stuffed animals speak in Mexican Spanish, and you have to read the rhinoceros book fourteen times a day. The rhinoceros book did not get lost, I hid it where no one would find it, among the unhung pictures in the hall closet, because I couldn't take it anymore. It must have stayed there until the move.

Sometimes I am also afraid of Maiko. Afraid of him. He comes down with every virus anybody at his preschool gets, he isolates and strengthens it within his snazzy new immune system and then attacks me with it as hard as he can. His colds demolish me, make me think I'm going to die, his stomach bugs bench me for a week at a time, his slight pink eye can blind me for two months. I see him coming toward me with his mucus, saying "papá," kind of crying, with that bubble of snot he gets in one of his nostrils, getting closer and closer to me, three-foot strep. My flesh and blood, my infectious little focus. He sticks his fingers in my mouth, the spoon he's sucked on, playing house, playing meals. He kills me. We were one body, because the monster was one and a trinity. The family body. Three organisms fused by a single circulatory system. Hence the terror that something might happen to any one of the three of us, since that would be like having a major part amputated.

Now Maiko is bigger, but at that time there were moments when I'd go into quasi-psychotic states, clutching my head when he cried, and nobody could calm him down. And that time he gave us lice, and that time with the subatomic diapers, remember? Not yet in control of his sphincters, the preschool report said. Shit all over everything. Arms coated up to the elbows trying to clean it up. The transition period, portable potties, accidents on the carpet, in the bathtub. Pure reality. And that involuntary superpower of his that lets him hit me in the balls from impossible angles. In the chair, in the bed, or playing any game, I'm across from him and his kick strikes with absolute precision, or his elbow, his throw that makes me double over. Sometimes he pauses before kicking the soccer ball, as if he's calculating all the variables of its trajectory, ballistics, gravity, and then the kick with the perfect aim at the very center of my suffering.

I worry most of all about the part that isn't funny. Maiko when he had fever seizures, and I thought he was going to die in my arms. Then the doctors explaining that it's totally normal for this to happen, that it's nothing serious. How can no one warn you about something like that? Maybe they just can't. If they offered a course on what it's like to raise kids, no one would have them. You need that ignorance in order for the species to continue, generations of ingénues who leap without even the remotest look. A course that would anticipate all the dangers and afflictions of paternity and maternity would frighten off everyone. It could be sponsored by some brand of condoms. You'd leave the classroom and go buy a pack of 120 without giving it a second thought.

I didn't go into the toy store. It'd be better to do it afterward when I had the money and more time in the afternoon. But I was going to have to get Maiko some kind of gift. Maybe in the duty-free on the way back. I was also going to get a good bottle of whiskey to celebrate. And a bottle of perfume for you, for putting up with me those past months. That was my rationale, my sensible decision: to be with you, tend our nest, our child. And yet sometimes you surrender to darker decisions, ones you make with your body, or that your body makes for you, the animal that you are. If you could see it, that would be one thing, but it can't be seen, it's a blind spot, outside of language, out of reach, and the crazy thing is that that's what we are, to a great extent, we're that beat that wants to perpetuate itself, because we know we'd decided to quit using protection, I remember it well, but months went by before you got pregnant, and how does the body decide? What changes? I'm almost certain you got pregnant after that night we argued at your apartment on Agüero, remember? For a minute it seemed like I'd go back to my place and like that would be that. "I'm not so sure," I told you, and I used the word "vertigo," saying I was afraid, and you were outraged. You were hurt by my hesitation, my restraint, you went to bed crying. I stayed in the living room for a little bit, not knowing what to feel, and then I went in to console you but still thinking I was leaving, and you said, "Stay today, you can go tomorrow," and we slept together, and at some point in the night we fucked in a way that was different, in a sort of battle between animals that are plunging deep into darkness, and that's where I remember the vertigo, surrendering to that vertigo when I came inside you, a liberating surrender, a total bravery, and may forces unknown to me decide, impulses, fluvial wills, cells, creatures, the fauna of the mystery, an orange dinosaur in a toy store.

I passed by some high schools (they call them "lyceums" here), they were just finishing their morning shift. Kids were coming out, shouting their goodbyes. From one side of the street to the other, one yelled to his friend in a superhero voice: "May nothing get in your way!"

I knew where that came from. I knew it was a catch-phrase from *Tremble, Ye Tyrants*, and I laughed because I got the joke and because I felt like I was on the inside of the interweaving of allusions and events. Back then, *Tremble, Ye Tyrants* was a viral hit. Every other week this guy would put out videos, with an affable voiceover, that people in Uruguay had uploaded over those two weeks. Little things, insignificant things: some kids removing a bird that had gotten into their house, for example, a girl riding a bike for the first time, a guy building a compressor out of a fridge . . . The result was a mix of tenderness, surprise, Uruguayana, third-world ingenuity, anthropological revelation. One Peteca, heavyset with a smile with no teeth in it, would appear every so often and repeat the sentence "May there be nothing in your way." And the video would always close by saying: "Which is why we give our thanks, YouTube, for everything you've given us." YouTube, like a divinity provider of the abundance of experience, intimacy, and human details. The smaller, inoffensive tone contrasted with the title, which is a quote from the national anthem: "The glory of this sacred gift/ We warranted: tremble, ye tyrants!"

The walk had made me hot, but I wanted to leave my jacket on because at the bank I was going to stash my money in the inside zip pocket. I passed some mildly frightening spots, a shopping arcade with dark shops. In front of one I was given a flyer that said: TATTOOS, tribal, goth, EXCELLENCE, safe, piercings, genital perforations. Again my associative constellation blazed. A person in love is like a person afflicted with severe paranoia: he thinks everything is speaking directly to him. The songs on the radio, movies, the horoscope, random street flyers . . . Guerra's piercing. At some point she'd gone into a place in the back of a shopping arcade and, with her legs open on a stretcher, received from someone a genital perforation, as the little gray piece of paper referred to it. A tattoo-artist friend? A person she could trust? With anesthesia? Did it hurt? In none of our e-back-and-forth had we brought up the subject. I put the flyer in my jacket pocket. I could have thrown it in any trash can instead of keeping it, and maybe if I had, what ended up happening would never have happened. But I kept it because I was interested in the language, the oscillation between "tú" and "vos," how when it said "You choose the design yourself," it mixed the local and the international grammars.

After the Plaza de los 33, the avenue curved. Who could that hero on horseback be? And then there was the big building, the Municipality Administration with a replica of the David on the esplanade. The two-way avenue, white taxis unlike our black-and-yellow cabs, buses, ANCAP "evolving for you," pharmacies, exchange offices, cash loans, Orion heaters ("the first with virgin copper tanks"), lottery offices, Magic Center, Motociclo, opticians, La Hora Exacta watch repair. I don't know what order I saw those things in, but I observed and absorbed them all as if it were the last day of my life. Expo Yi, the love locks fountain, La Papoñita, where I had once had coffee with Enzo, stands on the street, clothes, belts, peanuts, caramelized nuts, purses, wallets, the trees with their new leaves, some guys playing chess on top of some crates and others watching, among them a street sweeper taking a break leaning on his broom, the Delondon shopping center, a minibus with loudspeakers, "Check us out, charge your cell phone," Argentine magazines at the kiosks, traffic noise but not much honking, Parisien Indian, Galería 18. It all gets mixed up in my head even if I look at the streets on the map, since a few hours later Guerra and I walked those blocks on the other side, going the other way, totally wasted.

FOUR

There weren't many people at the bank. I got in the line for the cashiers. Up on the wall there was a TV to assuage the customers' anxieties. It was a sports program, someone interviewing Luis Suárez. You couldn't really hear it because they'd turned it way down, but they showed a few of his goals for Liverpool and Barça. Incredible shots with the gall of an angered bull, unstoppable and, with that remarkable capacity to penetrate matter, passing right through his rivals, the double nutmeg against the angel-faced Brazilian David Luiz, these goals coming clear from the middle of the field at maximum velocity, dematerializing the defenders, without that impossible diagonal of Messi's goals, more facing the goal and with a powerful kick. They left Suárez's little face in a corner of the screen as he watched his own goals. He was laughing with those enormous teeth of his, his eyes becoming slits.

His last contract with Barcelona had been for one hundred million dollars. And here I was, pleased to be about to take out fifteen grand—everything I had. What a chump. I couldn't wait to feel those crisp brand-new bills in my hands. I mentally went over my money again. Eight thousand dollars from Spain, seven thousand from Colombia. Exchanged on the Argentine black market at that time, that was around two hundred and forty thousand pesos. From an Argentine bank I'd get less than half that. This was the era of the dólar blue, the soybean dollar, the tourist dollar, the brick dollar, the official dollar, the future dollar . . . There were so many different exchange rates around I couldn't keep track. Nobody really knew how much things cost. The peso was going down, there was a lot of inflation. And they started trying to control exchange. It was like being paid in ice in the middle of the summer, and freezers were illegal. Everybody on a desperate search for dollars. The market split into official and parallel, and between them the cuevas popped up, the intermediaries, the friends of the cousins. That time they tried to rob me when I'd gone into the city center to exchange some cash, I called my cueva contact afterward. I told him: they followed me, they broke the window of my car, wanting to rob me. "I would put my hands in the fire for those guys," he told me, "they're my rugby friends." "Right, like the Puccios, you mean?" I asked him. He didn't laugh. But I think it was actually the parking-lot guys who already knew where the cuevas were and would target you. A medieval situation in the twenty-first century, a time of electronic transfers and virtual money, and here I was fetching some papers printed green from the other side of the river, hiding them, seeking some alternative, attempting to dodge the measures, the side effects of the State's determinations, finding that crack I could slip through.

I had a general idea of what I was going to do with the money. First I wanted to hold it in my hands. Then the fog would go, and I'd be able to see clearly. But in general I was planning on paying you back, paying the overdue bills, doing the repairs around the house, paying back my brother, getting a babysitter who would come over in the afternoon so I could get to work. Nine months or maybe even ten of working with tranquility, door shut, no interruptions. The novel for the Spanish publisher and the shorter pieces for Colombia. I owed two books. The shorter ones were almost done, I just had to figure out the structure of the book, put the pieces in order. The main thing was the novel. Ten months to write a novel. It wasn't bad. This was going to be my great novel. I could sense it. A guy who leaves his wife and kids and disappears in Brazil, transforms into somebody else. It was going to have moments in Portuñol, lots of wordplay, lots of verbal gunpowder, I was going to explode Spanish and then branch it out like a tree in every direction, a thousand things were going to happen, on the beach, in Brasilia, in the Amazon, lots of sex, and boats down huge rivers and contraband, drugs, shamans, shooting, wild parties, stories inside stories, it was going to be my *Ulysses*, my *Devil to Pay in the Backlands*, my total novel.

Just three more people, and it would be my turn. The security guard was slowly ambling around the bank with a step that was practically absent. Suárez was still being featured on the TV show. There was another guy I'm not sure wasn't "El Loco" Abreu, the one who scored that penalty goal in the 2010 World Cup against Ghana. You'd have to be really insane to try the Panenka right now, everybody thought, and then there he went, calm as a cucumber, out of the range of planetary nerves, he took one look at the ball, gained momentum, approaching with long strides and just when it seemed like he was going to shatter the ball, he chipped it, a lob into the blue, a parable of the devastating effect of slowness, an elegy to insanity, and the ball went in slowly, making a mockery of overwrought nutmegs, humiliating completely the goalie who had thrown himself to one side. Long standing ovation. Uruguay made it to the semifinals. I was very curious to know what Abreu was saying. Everyone in line was looking up at the screen.

At some point, without realizing it, all human beings became Rain Man. We cannot live without a screen. I don't ever go to the bathroom without my cell phone. It's this crippling fear of silence. Out of habit, you get more on board. Everybody with their mini TV in their hand. And since you aren't allowed to use your cell phone at the bank here, there's a screen on the wall. Now they were showing one from the archives where Suárez was around ten, on a kids' games program, he was supposed to overcome certain obstacles, jump down slides, climb. You could already see that desperate, competitive gall. Later he added skill.

What was my skill? Putting words together? Building elegant, expressive sentences? What did I know how to do, when all was said and done? Whenever I had earned some silver, what had it been in exchange for? Gathering words together on a sheet hadn't yielded me all that much cash. Teaching, a little bit more, perhaps. My seminars, my composition classes, my workshops. The trick with workshops is not to get too involved, not to dampen the literary enthusiasm, just let people make mistakes and figure it out on their own, encourage, guide, allow the group to go where it wants to go, let each member find whatever it is they're looking for and get to know themselves better. Something along those lines. For that they paid me at institutes and universities. But now it was different, now they were giving me money to sit down and write. And now I owed them. That debt was an invisible thing that was buried in my brain. A succession of narrated images that were supposed to emerge from my imagination. What I was supposed to pay that debt back with didn't exist, wasn't really anywhere. It had to be invented. My currency was a series of neural connections that would go about producing a verbal daydream. And if that narrative machine didn't work?

Silver, money, bills. When I was a kid my mom would give me "a red one and a blue one" for the school's refreshments stand. I didn't know how much that was. Bills back then were colors, not numbers. Ancient faces with watermarks. From the seventies to now, General San Martín has had to watch thirteen zeros pass through the corner of his eye. How much money had I cost my father? From my birth in the private hospital right up to the last few times I asked him for a loan, not long before his death. Since I showed up in the world I've been an endless procession of banknotes: room, board, soccer, English-language high school, uniforms, orthodontics, beach vacations, ski trips, trips to Europe, gifts, a horse, private university, gas, panels and paint after several car wrecks, a significant portion of our apartment on Coronel Díaz.

All that money that had shaped me, served as my entrance into a social group, a series of friends, a way of speaking, and that was curious, too: money had shaped my language. One time a couple of thugs had robbed my sister in a taxi, and when she was cursing them out one of them said to the other: "Man, that money really talks." That theft of consonants: "coacola" instead of "Coca-Cola," "again" instead of "against," "sparkplu" instead of "sparkplug," "too ien" instead of "todo bien" . . . The infinite codification of class. And the price of my Anglicism—how much had it cost to format the part of my brain that's in another language? That dream I had once about a guy who was screaming in the room next to mine and when I asked what was going on, they said: "They're taking out his English tongue."

There was money in my childhood, it surrounded me, it covered me in good clothing, provided me with blocks of a safe neighborhood in the city, picket fences on the weekends, soccer field fences, well-pruned privets, barriers that rose up on either side of me wherever I went. And I had subsequently taken the liberty of going off the rails, the artist with no business sense, the bohemian. Another liberty, another luxury. The sensitive child of the haute bourgeoisie. But the price of my Bohemia would have to be paid now. It was a long-term loan. A gradual slippage: a subtly justified switch in neighborhoods, a kid who wouldn't know snow, nor Europe, nor Disney World, and we'd have to put him in a different school when his tuition grew prohibitive, and soon enough he wouldn't be given the time of day at his first jobs, he'd belong but he wouldn't, he'd be semi-invited, always going swimming in other people's pools, inheriting the beat-up old car that ought to start all right. At twenty-five I had to learn to clean my own house, run the vacuum, scrub the bathroom, put my clothes in the wash, hang them up, cook twice a day, wash the dishes before going to bed. Live my life. Had that been good or bad? Now, at forty-four, it was bad, it was atrocious. That's how I figured it. I was tired, I wanted to have a cleaning lady, pay somebody by the hour, at least a babysitter for half the day so I could hole up and have a little time to write or simply pretend to be writing. I wanted to be alone, and it struck me then that solitude costs a lot of money, meant cleaning ladies doing the things I didn't want to do. I felt like a pauper among princes, the beggar of the gated communities, crashing others' wealth for a minute. I wanted my dollars, and I wanted them now. To write hearing somebody vacuuming in another room of the house and have it not be me. That seemed like a luxury to me. Who would have thought, when in my teenage years I had slept in while the cleaning lady vacuumed the hall outside my room and hit the door with the tube, again and again, so many of my awakenings happened that way, it was the call of the vacuums, *You'll see soon enough, Luqui, we'll be a part of your life soon enough, you'll really get to know us then.* Vacuum turbines blasting at full volume like a premonition.

I was next in line. I checked my pocket for my passport. It was one in the afternoon. I was this close to reaching my goal, a woman in a purple jacket was talking with the cashier, they knew each other, you could hear it all. I looked to see who was behind me. A guy in his fifties. And farther back there were more people. I was going to try to speak softly so they wouldn't be able to hear my request. There wasn't any partition to shield the activity at the counter. In Argentina they had made the banks cover up the counters so people wouldn't be able to tell how much money you were withdrawing. That was after a pregnant woman had been shot coming out of the bank with the cash for some real estate transaction, since in Argentina you have to buy houses and apartments in cash. I can't think what her name was. They blamed the bank, the cashier was a suspect . . . it was the most shocking in a succession of violent robberies like that of people leaving banks, and they ended up putting in those partitions to shield the counters. Here it was all just exposed.

The woman in the purple jacket left.

"Next," said the cashier.

I went up and spoke, kind of crouching down through the opening money was handed through.

"I'd like to take out fifteen thousand dollars," I said, almost in a whisper, passing her my passport.

"Tell me over here," she said, pointing to a kind of round speaker right in front of her face.

I said it again as quietly as I could.

"Fifteen thousand?" she said, and it sounded pretty loud.

I nodded. She looked at my passport, looked something up on her computer. She left her station, went to talk to another employee in one of the cubicles. They looked at me. The other employee said something. The cashier came back.

"Normally withdrawals of more than ten thousand dollars have to be done at our central headquarters, unless you let the branch know in advance. But we can make an exception, okay?"

"Oh, I didn't know that, thanks."

She had me sign the receipt, she checked my signature, she left her post again. She went in the back and disappeared behind a door. There was too much happening. She came back with a wad, put it in the electric bill counter. The machine made a horrific, whistleblowing noise. She put a rubber band around the wad and when she was about to hand it to me, I said:

"Could you exchange five hundred into Uruguayan?"

"Sure."

She exchanged them for me, gave me the pesos, which I put in my pants pocket, and then the wad of dollars, which I put in the inside pocket of my jacket. I zipped up my jacket, said muchas gracias, turned and darted out of the bank without looking anybody in the eye.

Done. I was loaded. I thought of Guerra. That was the first thing I thought about. A sum of possibilities in that wad of cash I could feel against my heart. A sort of opening in all possible directions. Master of time. Time was mine. Almost a whole year in my pocket. I could do what I wanted. That's why I thought of Guerra. That strength also came with fear. The fear of the prey in the jungle. I had paranoia on my heels. I quickened my step, cut across the Plaza del Entrevero down its diagonal path, jaywalked across the avenue and went into La Pasiva.

There were a lot of people there around lunchtime. I found an empty table by the wall and sat down, almost at the very back, facing the door. I saw your message on my cell: *How's it going?* I wrote you back: *It's done.* But I took a minute to send it. I erased it, and then I wrote it again, and then I sent it. My battery was down to about half. I tried to find an outlet to plug in the charger, but the plug was for two little round pegs, and mine were flat, and there were three of them. I didn't have an adapter. A waiter came up to me in a black vest, very dapper, looking a little like Alfredo Zitarrosa.

"Sir," he said, like that, without a question mark.

"A half-pint of Pilsen, if you would."

I waited. I'd be meeting Guerra in a different place, by the water, along the promenade. Here I was killing time, mixing with people in a safe place. I wondered if it was safer to leave the bank and go inside a restaurant, or just walk around and go into a building every so often, a hotel or wherever, to give them the slip. The waiter brought me my beer.

"Thanks."

"Not at all," he said.

I took stock of the faces of everyone who came in. I fantasized about a guy coming in and heading straight for my table, whispering, "Hand it over, and no harm will come to you," barely opening his jacket to show me the gun, and I would hand it over without batting an eye, the guy would leave: the perfect heist. I took two sips of my beer. I took my backpack and went to the bathroom.

I went into one of the stalls, but it didn't lock, so I went into a different one, which also didn't. Both locks had been busted. I backed up against the door so no one could come in and got my travel money belt out of my back-pack. Quickly I stuck the wad of dollars inside it, zipped it up and put it around my waist. I undid my pants. The money was against my crotch. I tightened the elastic and did my pants back up over it. Now I was like a mule trying to get drugs across the border. I looked at my reflection and smoothed out my clothes. I looked like I had a bit of a belly, but with the sweater and the loose t-shirt, it didn't stand out. It was safer than going around with the money in my jacket.

When I came out of the bathroom and returned to my table I noticed that the belt was somewhat uncomfortable. Sitting down, the wad pressed into my thighs. Regardless, I stayed that way, figuring things would adjust, that I'd get used to it. The restaurant's radio was playing some very eighties tunes: Guns N' Roses, the Eagles, and one song I've always hated that says something about "toy soldiers," I don't know whose it is, but it reminds me of a girlfriend I had in high school who used to listen to it on repeat. I took a look at the menu. All of it made me hungry, the special chivitos, the chajá for dessert. Their logo was a blond kid eating a huge hot dog, sitting on a barrel that said La Pasiva. I've always found that image funny. Wouldn't somebody have opened up a chain of restaurants in Montevideo called La Activa? The beer was cheering me up, putting me at ease. I emptied the glass with a couple of large swigs. All the ills of the world had healed over. I motioned to the waiter, paid my check and went outside.

FIVE

I was all in. In the best sense. I could feel it when the sun shone on my face. I had taken the necessary precautions. Now all I had to do was surrender to the rhythm of the day. I relaxed and enjoyed the walk. I was going to meet a woman. There's nothing better than that. All around me it was a beautiful blue September day.

I got to Plaza Independencia, where the monument to Artigas barely cast a shadow. There were a couple of disoriented Brazilians looking at a map. I thought I recognized them from the ferry. The man was muscular, with skin the color of café con leche and a baseball cap; the woman had recently been to the hairdresser's, and she was wearing tight jeans over her powerful thighs, and big earrings. They were pointing up at something behind me when I passed by. I walked a couple more steps and turned around. There was the Palacio Salvo. Gigantic. Guerra had sent me a link to the solo album by the singer from

Blur that had on its cover a picture of that old building, half Art Deco and half Gothic. It has a twin on Avenida de Mayo in Buenos Aires, the Palacio Barolo. Both of them have a tower with a lighthouse. At some point those two lighthouses used to send each other signals, they were like an entrance portal to the River Plate. There it was, impressive. But the album cover showed it from another angle. From above, maybe from a taller building. I looked around. They must have taken the picture from a high floor of that tower, the Radisson. That was the instant serendipity of associations: I looked at the Brazilians who were looking at the building, and it was identical to the one in the picture that Guerra had sent me that had been taken from the Radisson for the cover of a CD. With those ricochets, my mind clambered up to that high floor. And my desire climbed with it. I could do it. Why not? I crossed the street and went inside the hotel.

There were few people in the lobby. Marble floor, leather armchairs, high ceiling, smooth surfaces, the empty space of luxury, that international air. At reception I was helped by a young guy who could see I was a little trepidatious.

"How can I help you today, señor?"

"Good afternoon, I was just wondering how much a room would cost on the . . . How many floors do you have?"

"There are rooms up to the twenty-fourth floor."

"On the twentieth floor, facing the plaza, how much would it be?"

"One bed?"

"Yes."

"Two hundred and forty dollars a night."

I looked at him, I thought it was going to be more expensive. I thought the exorbitant price was going to decide for me, foreclosing the possibility.

"Great, I'll take it," I said.

"Just one person?"

"Yes."

"And if I could just have your credit card, please."

"If I pay you up front in cash do you need the card?"

"No, if you pay for it now I would not need the card."

I had a hard time getting the money out of my belt. I made some suspicious maneuvers. The man was watching me, he couldn't see what I was doing with my hands on the other side of the counter, trying to loosen my pants. I must have looked to him like I was about to take a piss right there. I gave him my passport and paid him with three hundred-dollar bills.

I went up to Room 262. I liked the number. I opened the door. I put my backpack on the bed and pulled back the curtain. The view from that height! The strange tower of the Palacio Salvo, the horizon of the river in the background. I was living my life. Enough sublimating into literature, making up stories. I wanted to live. To see, to touch. To get inside reality. Get inside Guerra. Get into a war with my fucking imagination, my eternal invisible world. I sat down on the bed. I checked how well it bounced. I wanted to hold her naked there, her real body with me. That was the bed where I would finally go from thought to action. You had already done it, you went over to the other side of the mirror every now and then, brought back smells, moods, opinions, laughter, echoes of an intimacy that I didn't know; then you dreamed alone by my side. I also dreamed alone. In that moment, sitting there in that empty room, I was like a director scoping out locations for a movie I'd never get to make.

I left nothing in the room but a huge biography of Rimbaud, six hundred pages, which I'd brought to finish reading and hadn't even opened yet. It was just weighing down my backpack. It got left on that bedside table. I went to the bathroom and took a long, foamy piss. With all my nervousness about the money, I hadn't realized I had to go. I washed my hands and my face. I looked in the mirror. I fixed my hair a little, it had been squashed down by those hours on the bus. That was my face; as always, I felt somehow unreal. I said, "Vamos Pereyra." Let's go. Before leaving the room, I took a picture from the window. It was ten to two.

I crossed the plaza and went down toward the water along a street that ran behind the Solís Theatre. Again the dark purple horizon of the open river, or a piece of it, at least. I had the intuition of a poem, but I didn't write it down, and now I can't remember what it was I hoped to say. Perhaps it was merely beer-infused enthusiasm, nerves. But I went with a diaphanous spirit, intuiting a celestial, atmospheric poem, in the intimate glare of a Montevideo that was largely deserted. I remembered that poem by Borges about Montevideo where he talks about the piety of a slope. "My heart slides down the evening like weariness down the piety of a slope." Later he edited it and put: "I slide down your evening like weariness . . ." I guess the sliding heart struck him as over the top in the end, almost a butcher's shop image, a bolero image (in fact "heart" is one of the words he removed most often in his edits). I like that intimate second person at the beginning, he's speaking almost in secret to the city: I slide down your evening. He also struck two lines in their entirety. The first said: "You are still and pellucid in the evening like the memory of a friendship that was flush." Something bothered him, the repetition of "evening," the two adjectives that were a little stilted: "pellucid," "flush." And the other one he took out said: "Love sprouts from your stony surface like a humble lawnlet." It might have struck him as too sentimental, too precious, that diminutive, "lawn" too close to "lamb." But I liked the poem. It talks about the Uruguayan capital as a Buenos Aires of the past. "You are ours and frolicsome, like the star the water doubles," it says. "Frolicsome," although it's used less commonly these days because it has erotic implications, continues to be a good word. It has some Candombe in it. And the doubled air of Montevideo; the same but different, swaying in reflection. Then he talks about the sunrise, the sun that rises over the turbid water. And he ends with the line: "Streets with the light of a patio." A simple line, short, effective after those longer ones, capturing the affable, familiar air of those low buildings, the idealized hospitality of Montevideo. At some point over the course of the year, magnetized by long-distance love, I had learned the poem by heart, and as I was doing that, I'd discovered the differences between the two versions.

I saw from afar the Santa Catalina restaurant with its yellow awnings. I went by a construction site with a half-demolished building, its walls graffitied, crossed the street and entered. There were a couple of customers having lunch. Guerra wasn't there yet. I said hello and selected a table outside, facing the direction she'd be coming from. President Mujica came to eat here sometimes, it was said. It was near the Executive Tower and was a place that suited Mujica's simple, popular style: an old restaurant, unpretentious, with aluminum chairs on the sidewalk and honest meals. It was lovely in the shade of that awning, Cata, in that establishment that took its name from your saint, waiting for a woman I had seen all of twice. The first time in January and the second at that very restaurant, in March.

An older man came up to me from inside. This time I initiated:

"How's it going?"

"Can't complain. You?" he asked as he wiped my clean table.

"Excellent. Nice day for a beer."

"What kind can I bring you?"

"A big bottle of Pilsen and a couple of glasses."

"You're waiting for someone, I take it?"

"Waiting on a lady."

"Marvelous. Will you be dining with us today?"

"Most likely."

"Even better," he said and went inside.

The last time, when I went to open the bank account, Guerra and I had a few beers at that same table. I told her my economic microplan, that I was going to be traveling a few times a year to get money, that we could meet up each time. She kept my advances at bay. She said: "There are many pairs of eyes in Montevideo." She laughed. That day I had to go back through Colonia, taking a bus that left early from Tres Cruces station, so we were only able to spend a little while together. We didn't even kiss. But we talked a lot. She told me that she was living with her boyfriend in the Nuevo París neighborhood, that she was still with the newspaper, that she rode her bike to work. She talked about her mother's illness, a bone marrow cancer that took her quickly. She didn't get along with her father, and she had a brother who lived in the United States. That time I took a book to give her, but not one of mine: Herzog's diaries from when he was filming *Fitzcarraldo*. She told me she had looked for my books in Montevideo but hadn't found any. She had read a couple of things online, and she said she liked them. I don't remember what else we talked about. I know I promised her I'd be back soon, and I hadn't kept that promise because only now, six months later, had I returned.

A pregnant woman appeared on the other side of the street, with a big round stomach. Was that Guerra? It looked like her. She got closer, but then she crossed diagonally, and once I could see her better, I realized it wasn't Guerra after all. She kept going, but my heart continued bucking like it was trying to dodge a knife. For a moment I thought she was going to show up like that, with a big belly. It was possible. Although maybe she would have said something in an email. I fantasized about her showing up pregnant, and we would take a walk, get some ice cream, sit down every so often for her to rest. I'd go with her to look at baby things. It couldn't be mine, that I could be certain of. I fantasized that, pregnant, she would want to fuck regardless; we'd go to the hotel room. I made up a whole movie that was very tender, her naked with her belly, beautiful, her breasts bigger. I felt aroused. I don't even have a thing for pregnant women in general, yet suddenly I felt I could have been with her like that. You were beautiful, too, when you were pregnant.

The waiter brought me the beer, put the cloth over his shoulder, went to the curb to get out from under the awning and stood staring at the sky in the direction of the promenade. I could tell he wanted to chat.

"Think the president might come today?"

"Oh, El Pepe hasn't been here in a while."

I filled my glass. He kept staring in the same direction as if searching for something in the distance.

"Storm coming?" I asked him.

"No, not a storm. Aliens," he said, smiling.

"Oh yeah?"

"There was a light out there yesterday, over the river."

"A spaceship?"

"I don't know what it was. It was glimmering, it had a diamond shape, like this."

He made a shape with his hands that I couldn't quite make out. I wasn't sure if he was serious. I asked, warily: "Did it move?"

"No, it was still. A pinkish light. You could see it crystal clear. It must have been four or five kilometers away. It was big."

"Well . . . sometimes strange things happen," I said.

"I had never seen anything like that."

It didn't seem like he was joking.

"Everybody who was here saw it, but they didn't say anything about it on TV or in the papers."

"Did people get scared?"

"Nah. It was more the unexpectedness of it. We all looked at it awhile, and then just as suddenly as it had come, it was gone."

"You hadn't had anything to drink that could have . . . ?"

"Water," he said, with a straight face.

"Maybe it was the Virgin."

"Nah, how could it be if none of us here are religious."

"You don't have to be religious," I said. "Besides, aren't the Virgin and the aliens the same thing?"

"I wouldn't know about that," he said. He didn't want to speculate. Neither did I.

I asked him how old the restaurant was, who the chef was, what kind of food it was known for, what he'd recommend. Roast lamb with potatoes and sweet potatoes, ravioli with a little tomato sauce, their stews . . . I was hungry for it all.

"As soon as the lady arrives, we'll order."

"Very good," he said, heading back inside.

"If anything appears in the sky, I'll let you know."

"Deal."

It was a quarter past two, and there was no sign of Guerra. I considered the possibility that she wouldn't show. There was a part of me that almost would have preferred it that way. That way I could have left, with an aura of someone abandoned yet not quite rejected, free from humiliation, almost victorious, the encounter declared null and void. I could say to myself: she didn't show. She didn't keep the appointment. And that would have prevented me from getting into any trouble. It would have freed me from trickery and lies. I could have remained on this side. Instead of crossing lines, passing the point of no return. It would have been a way of not taking responsibility, I guess. A ploy, in a way, not to have to decide for myself, to leave it up to the elemental particles of chaotic becoming. My heart was pounding. There was still time to flee. For a moment I considered that, too. Get up, pay, and go without looking back, leave along the promenade, take a walk and kill time until my visit to Enzo in the evening. A clean break. An emailed apology afterward. And I could be calm and alone, and think, focus on my novel, sit in some other café on 18 de Julio . . . Suddenly the meeting made me panic. What was I going to talk about? How was I going to convince her to come to the hotel with me? I was a little tired now, I was hungry. Didn't have much energy. What if she agreed to go to the hotel, and I couldn't get it up because I was nervous and tired, and there were too many expectations? What if her boyfriend came instead of her and beat the shit out of me? Or just gave me a dressing down. "You Lucas Pereyra?" My friend Ramón had that happen once. He'd made a date in front of a telo with a girl who had a boyfriend. They'd hooked up two or three times before. Suddenly as he's waiting a guy comes up and says: "You Ramón?" "Yes." "I'm Laura's boyfriend. Don't worry, I'm not going to hit you. But if you try getting in touch with Laura again, I'll have to kill you. Deal?" "Deal," Ramón said, and the guy went on his way. My friend told me the guy wasn't particularly big, but he had a decisive and controlling attitude that terrified him. Of course he didn't see the girl ever again; he didn't tell her what happened, either. I figured that if Guerra's boyfriend—that guy I saw in Valizas when she got off the bus—found out he'd be less disposed to have a conversation. But I hadn't actually done anything, I'd just invited her for lunch. Up until this point it was all completely on the up and up.

Out of the corner of my eye I saw a dog with the muzzle and someone jammed two fingers into the back of my neck. I jumped and bumped the table and knocked over my glass, which was fortunately almost empty. It was Guerra, coming from the promenade, with a dog. She was different; I almost didn't recognize her.

"Hey handsome, don't be scared," she said into my ear, giving me a little squeeze. "I have to go to the bathroom, hold him for me, will you?"

She handed me the leash, righted my beer glass and disappeared inside the restaurant. The flash of her back, the blue apple of her ass in jeans. It all happened in five seconds. An earthquake. I stood there holding the leash. The dog looked at me like it was embarrassed. The muzzle looked like more of a punishment than a preventative measure. It was a black pit bull with a white patch on its chest. A shy pit. Both of us made uncomfortable by this forced introduction. The dog took another look at me, lowered its eyes, and sat down. Then I sat down, too.

SIX

We can't go to a hotel with a dog. That was my first thought. Less still with that dog. Years and years of genetic manipulation had edged it toward what it was today: a jaw of a dog, rough, tough, a canine cudgel of lethal chomps, a Tasmanian devil with a huge square head. The muzzle canceled its very essence. It was a handcuffed Tyson. Every now and then it gave me a glance.

Who would want a dog like that? What emotional vacuum was a monster like this supposed to fill, in a home? Was it a metaphor for something? For what? What was it an extension of? Double animal, nagual—whose? Why the fuck was this chick bringing me her boyfriend transformed into a dog, leaving me to tend to him? Or was the dog watching me? I poured beer into the two glasses. And Guerra showed up. She was gorgeous, my God.

"You're thinner, Pereyra," she said as she sat down.

"You're different, too. Didn't you change your hair?"

"I got rid of my flex."

"Your what? Your bangs?"

"We call it a flex here."

"It looks good on you. You're more sort of . . ."

"More what?"

"Less of a kid."

"You mean it makes me look older?"

"No, it makes you look like a woman. Not a little girl. It looks great." We looked at each other for a moment in silence, smiling.

"Want to pass me Cuco?" she said.

"Cuco's its name?

"Yep. He's a bit of a monster, isn't he?"

"A bit . . . He won't run off?"

"No, but tie him to the chair just in case."

I got up and tied the leash around the chair leg. "There we go. Does he bite?"

"No, he's very easygoing. But for a couple of years now these kinds of dogs, fighting dogs, have been required to wear muzzles in public."

"Such an organized country, Uruguay. Is he your boyfriend's dog?"

"Yeah, but no."

"What do you mean?"

"Yeah, the dog is his, but no, he's not my boyfriend anymore." (I'm not a Peronist, but sometimes you've just got to shout, at the top of your lungs, silently of course, keeping your poker face: *Long live Perón!*)

"So what are you doing with the dog?"

"A friend is going to take care of him, until he gets back from a tour."

The waiter arrived. He asked Guerra what she wanted to eat.

"What are you having?" she asked me.

"I'll have that lamb with the potatoes and the boñatas. What was the word? They're sweet potatoes, right?"

"Boñato," she corrected me. Lots of little things had different names in Uruguay.

"That," I said.

"I'll have the same," said Guerra.

The waiter went back inside to put in our order. I raised my glass.

"It's good to see you, Guerra."

"Same, Pereyra." We clinked our glasses.

For a moment I thought: Who is this person? She was like a total stranger. It was hard to match her to my months-long delirium. I don't mean she wasn't good-looking—in fact, in those jeans and that t-shirt, which was kind of open in the back, she was hot as hell—but the ghost of Guerra that had been with me all that time was so powerful that I found it strange that this was really her, here, before my very eyes.

"What happened with your boyfriend?"

"The latest Uruguayan epidemic happened."

"What?"

"The worst part is that it was my idea. They raised our rent by quite a bit at his place, so I asked my friend Rocío—the one with the publishing house, remember, from Valizas?"

"Yeah . . ."

"I asked her if she wanted to rent a place with us because she'd been looking for something."

"Mmmm . . . What had she been looking for, exactly? This can't end well."

"Wait. We each paid a third of the rent. Things were going well: we cooked together, we took turns cleaning, plus she'd occasionally leave us alone because she went to her mom's quite often . . . The ideal situation."

"Did she and your boyfriend get along?"

"No. César said he couldn't stand her."

(First time I'd heard her boyfriend's name: César. I looked at the dog. He'd fallen asleep under the table.)

"She would hole up in her room, she wasn't one to be out with us having tea or watching television. She'd grab these cookies, take a couple, then go back to her room with her yerba mate to read."

"The perfect roommate," I said.

"The perfect bitch. Little miss prim and proper who couldn't get a boyfriend, didn't want to go dancing or anything else. One day I'm airing out her room a little, and I start sweeping, my plan was to freshen her sheets, and that's when I saw it: a short gray hair. Rocío doesn't have short gray hair. César does."

"That's horrible," I said.

"Horrrrrrible. I was stunned, but then I started putting the pieces together, and I worked out the whole thing: all the times they'd been alone together when I hadn't been there, the way César would put off leaving the house so I'd go out first, even the seemingly bad vibes between them took on this new meaning—it was awkwardness!"

"That made it seem like they didn't like each other."

"Yeah!"

"But wait," I said, "because . . . and sorry for saying this: I didn't see your friend in that much detail, but it's not like she's some irresistible goddess."

"She's not at all. She's ugly! That's exactly what I screamed at César. I still can't get my head around it. Obviously I wouldn't have put some bombshell in my house to get my boyfriend's dick hard. Rocío was my friend, low profile, no curves, no tits at all, super quiet, practically a spinster, this little bookworm . . . The problem is you guys will hump anything that moves."

"Don't lump me in with him."

"Men don't fuck their sisters because their sisters won't let them, otherwise they would. Mothers, too."

"Okay . . . Let's get back to this man in particular. Did you confront him?"

"First I wanted to be sure."

"What did you do?"

"I recorded them."

"No. Seriously? How?"

"One Saturday morning, Rocío was taking a shower, and I left my cell phone under her bed, recording. César was listening to music in our room. I told him I was heading into the city center for a bit for a meeting about the movie."

"What movie?"

"I'm working on a movie."

"That's so great."

"I agree, very salty."

"You're acting?"

"No, I'm in production. But wait, I'll tell you about that after. The point is I left. I went back at noon, waited for Rocío to go to her mom's place and got out my cell."

"It was there, they hadn't found it?"

"No, I'd put it on silent: it keeps recording, but it's basically off. I put in my headphones and told César I was going to take Cuco for a walk."

Guerra fell silent.

"And?"

She didn't say anything, just made a little movement with her head, like a mini no. Suddenly she spoke, her voice cracking. I'm terrified of women crying. I thought: How did I get mixed up in this Venezuelan soap opera? How do I come back from this? What does the manual say for cases like these?

How do you seduce a girl who's crying and has her boyfriend's dog? That's my first reaction when a woman cries, my brain flees as far as possible, to the very bottom of my selfishness, to the other end of grief and love, I plan out my escape, and only then do I start to return, little by little, I become soothing, perhaps because the crying finally has its intended effect on me.

"I never thought . . . I swear, I never thought," Guerra said with tears in her eyes. Her face sort of melted. "He said the same things to her that he said into my ear when we were in bed!"

"What things?"

"No, I'm not going to tell you, it's very intimate, but he said identical things to her."

"That's so awful, Guerra. It isn't good to have that much information. You shouldn't have recorded them."

"But they would have denied it to my face. And I wanted to know the truth."

"Sometimes the truth is too much."

"No, I prefer it this way. This way, you know what? I'll never see the son of a bitch again."

"Where are you living?"

"With my dad."

"Didn't you not get along with your dad?"

"I still don't, but we never even see each other."

Suddenly I felt very affectionate toward her and wanted to protect her. I wanted to hold her. But there was the table in between us. I seized her hand between the glasses, like a tender arm-wrestling match, I kissed her fist.

"You're going to be okay," I told her.

She nodded. She used her hands to dry her tears. I handed her a packet of tissues, and she blew her beautiful nose.

"Let's order whiskey," she said.

They brought us the lamb, and I ordered two J&Bs on the rocks.

"How are you?" she asked me.

"I'm fine. But finish the story. What did you do after that?"

"Oh my god, what I did after that was pretty outrageous. I overdid it a little, but it's done now. I went back and said nothing, I just went to sleep. That night some kiddies were coming over. They started showing up at eight. More and more of them . . . so I waited. Once everyone was there, I told them I was going to put some music on, and on the big speakers I put on the audio of them having sex right at the worst moment, when she was screaming 'Fuck me harder, fuck me harder.'"

"Are you serious? What about the kids?"

"What kids?"

"The kiddies who were there."

"No, 'kiddies' means 'friends' in Uruguay. People my age."

"Ah! Still. That's crazy."

"I know, but it was worth it. Their faces! You could even hear him spanking her. Nobody could figure out what was going on. Some of them were laughing. César went up to the speakers, disconnected my phone and threw it against the wall. He didn't even look at me, he just went to the door and as he was leaving I said: 'Yeah, get the fuck out of here. And you may as well get out, too,' I said to Rocío.

She burst into tears. Our friends had figured it out by then, but they didn't know who to console. I was standing there, waiting for her to leave, when suddenly she says: 'We were going to tell you tomorrow: I'm pregnant.'"

"What?!"

"Exactly what you heard," said Guerra. "The snake is pregnant."

They brought us our whiskeys, and we downed them quickly. That pregnancy changed everything. I didn't know what to say to her. We started eating.

"Were you able to take care of your errands?" she asked me.

"Yeah, that's done."

"Good," said Guerra.

I don't know if it was because I was very hungry or what, but that lamb was one of the most delicious dishes I've had in my whole life. It was prepared with rosemary, the potatoes and sweet potatoes cut kind of big, these crispy wedges. I sat back in my chair, relaxed. Under the awning there was a patio light—Borges had been right. I watched Guerra eat. It felt like my odds had improved. Maybe she wanted revenge sex, to restore her self-esteem. But I needed to be careful not to overplay my role as a shoulder to cry on, since I could get sucked down into a whirlpool. The biggest problem was still the dog. I ordered two more whiskeys.

I pulled up the picture I'd taken from the window of the hotel room.

"Look, Guerra," I said and handed her my phone. She put down her knife and fork and took it.

"The Palacio Salvo?"

"Yeah, I just took that photo in the hotel."

"At the Radisson? Look at you, Pereyra! You're doing pretty well these days."

"I got a room so we could be alone."

"You've got it all planned out."

"Yeah."

"And how long has this plan been in the works?

"Since I saw you dancing in Valizas."

"Well, look at you . . ."

I leaned in, and she leaned in to hear what I was going to tell her in a low voice:

"I want to be in bed with you. See you naked. Cover you in kisses."

I watched her mouth. The number of things that crossed that mouth in two seconds. She kind of bit her lips, almost puckered them, curled them to one side, smiled.

"I have a friend who works reception at the Radisson. She could see me. I told you that Montevideo's full of eyes."

"What do you care? You don't have a boyfriend anymore."

I had phrased that poorly. She recoiled in her chair. The intimacy I had fostered broke. I wanted to fix it:

"You can tell your friend you have to do an interview for the paper."

"Who writes these scripts of yours, dude?"

I laughed, I sat back in my chair, too. It wasn't going to be easy.

"Forget about that graybeard."

"That graybeard is younger than you are. How old are you?"

"Forty-four."

"He's thirty-eight, ten older than me."

"An old man! How does he have all that gray hair? He isn't doing too good."

"I like my men worn in, just like my jeans."

"I'm at death's door, in that case. Totally destroyed."

At least I made her laugh, but she regained her footing swiftly:

"You've just been spoiled by life," she said. "You're a Peter Pan who never wants to grow up. That's why you don't age."

"That's because I'm waiting for you. I sleep in a freezer like Walt Disney in order to wait for you."

"You won't be attracted to me when I'm forty."

"Let's do a little test. A friend of mine came up with this. I'm going to name a character, and you tell me the actor that first comes to your mind. Deal?"

"Sure."

"Batman."

"Um . . . Val Kilmer."

"Good!"

"What does that prove?"

"That we can be together."

"Because . . . ?"

"According to this rule, you can't go out with someone if there's a difference of more than two Batmans. To me, Batman is Adam West, the psychedelic one with the light blue leggings from the seventies."

"What other ones are there? Val Kilmer . . ."

"Michael Keaton, the one from *American Psycho*, what's his name?"

"Christian Bale."

"That's the one. If you had said Christian Bale, our affair could never have been. There'd be a difference of too many Batmans. That would mean different worlds, imaginations that don't coincide at any point. Every single thing one person says the other imagines in a completely different way."

"Do you really think it's like that?"

"No."

The money belt was getting extremely uncomfortable. I tried to move it up a little, so it wouldn't gouge me in the groin. What did I want all that money for if I couldn't have Guerra? I just wanted to make her fall in love. She hadn't shown the least bit of interest in going to the hotel with me, so I decided I couldn't keep pushing. It wasn't going to help me win her over. I needed to let our time together flow, flower. The afternoon. The conversation. The alcohol. I needed to loosen up a little, like they say. Not annoy her by bringing it up again . . .

"Shall we go to the Radisson, Guerra? We can order champagne to the room. If you don't want to, we don't have to do anything. We can just take a nap. I'll spoon you."

"Lucas . . ."

"What, Magalí? Maga, you're La Maga. I'd never thought of that, and you're Uruguayan, just like Cortázar's La Maga, from *Hopscotch*!"

"Lucas, seriously. Can we have a serious conversation?"

"Yes."

"You send me an email out of the blue saying you're coming, you suddenly show up, you want us to race off to a hotel and have sex, and then you're off to catch the ferry to go back . . ."

"You're right, and I'm being clumsy, it's just I don't have much time."

"Well, of course you don't have much time, you don't have much time here, because your time is elsewhere, with your wife and your child. You're from a completely different time."

I looked at her.

"I'm down for the count, Guerra. That was Uruguayan Taekwondo. That was a knockout."

She studied me to see how I took it, watched me gradually absorb the effect of her words.

"Uruguayan Taekwondo," I said, "is Taekwondo but with a thermos under your arm, am I right? All the martial arts are like that here: thermos and mate in one hand, offense and defense with the other. Extreme sports, too. Bungee jumping with a thermos. Even the surgeons here operate with a thermos . . ."

"Are you hearing what I'm saying?"

"Yes . . . I heard you say something about time."

Guerra's face remained serious.

"I heard you," I said, "I'm making jokes out of sheer patheticness, to negate my demise. If I've got to go, I at least want to make my executioners laugh on my way out."

"I loved what happened in Valizas, our walk to Polonio," Guerra said. "I was really into you. But then we didn't see each other. I can't afford to just go to Buenos Aires. And you only show up from time to time. We'll get involved again, you'll leave again, we'll spend months sending each other little emails, you'll show up next year . . . I'm hurt right now, I don't want any more pain. And that's not because I'm scared you'll hurt me, it's because I don't want any pain, I don't want to miss you. I don't want to miss you."

"You're right," I said, looking her in the eye, and I raised my glass with its half-melted remains of ice. "A final round?"

"Sure, a final round."

We ordered some more whiskey. Cuco was snoring, stretched out over the big cool stone tiles.

SEVEN

But the final round wasn't the final round. There were a couple more. It was my treat, I paid a ton of money without any idea of the exact amount, since with my undulating math I found it impossible to calculate the exchange rate with that currency. Bills featuring the face of the poet Juana de Ibarbourou. Another with a portrait of the painter Figari, one of his paintings of a dance on the flip side. Artists on banknotes, rather than war heroes. Will there ever be a bill with Borges on it?

We walked with Mr. Cuco (I started calling him that because I started getting along with him better). Guerra asked if I would walk her to her friend's place, where she'd be leaving him. Something eased between us as we walked together, shoulder to shoulder, now that we weren't facing each other down, across the table. It was a relief to move along, taking in the day, the two of us. I remember that on the corner I saw her back, in that short t-shirt that opened up behind her.

"Is this a bikini?" I said, tugging slightly on the horizontal elastic of her light green bra.

"Fft!" she swatted me away. "It's a sports bra." Walking next to her, I put my arm around her waist and squeezed.

"That's how I grabbed you in Valizas that night."

"Oh, I remember. Pretty bold."

We had a somewhat restricted personal mythology. Just a few anecdotes together. But we made them count. I don't know what street we took. Even looking at the map now I can't find it, but it must have been one that ran parallel to the promenade. We sang "Sweetness in the Distance," badly, forgetting parts. In tune enough, though, the both of us, especially in the last verse of, "My destiny has flown away. My life has gone by in just instants, a crossroads at the end of a day. And your sweetness in the distance." Although sometimes we'd get the last line mixed up with "crickets' songs were constants," from the previous verse. At some point I stuck my hand in my jacket pocket and found the flyer from the tattoo parlor.

"Wow," I said. "Genital perforations!"

Guerra looked at the paper.

"What is this?"

"Somebody gave it to me when I was walking down the 18 de Julio."

"Just 18," she says. "Nobody says 'the 18.'"

"Sorry, sorry. I had no intention of breaking the rules of the Montevidean sociolect! I'm going to get a genital perforation. That way my cock can communicate with your piercing, through telepathy."

Guerra started laughing.

"I'd like to see it again."

"What would you like to see again?"

"Your esteemed piercing."

"You didn't see it before."

"Well . . ."

"No, you didn't see it."

"Right, I guess I didn't meet it face to face. But I felt it. I had it sizzling against my fingers."

The most beautiful smile in the world. A dirty smile, surreptitious and complicit.

"There's a room waiting for us," I told her. "How far is your friend's house? Let's let this dog loose right here and just go. We'll take off his muzzle, we'll release him once and for all, may he run free and dine upon all the children in the plazas. Free Mr. Cuco!"

She had a kind of heroic air about her, Guerra, walking that dog that was dragging her forward by the leash. A Homeric goddess with her mastiff.

"I'm going to get a tattoo that says 'Mr. Cuco' on my shoulder. Seriously."

"You are not getting a tattoo. You don't have any, do you?"

"No. But seriously, I want to get one."

"Like what?"

"A flower," I said. "Maybe a rose petal with a piercing."

"How poetic. Your wife will love it."

"Yeah. Or I'll get a tattoo that says 'Guerra' here on one shoulder and on the other I'll put 'Paz.' War and peace! Why not?"

"Is your wife's name Paz?"

"No."

That was all I told Guerra about you, Catalina. I didn't say one word more. There was a certain loyalty in my disloyalty. And I was very drunk. All of this was happening as we were jaywalking, in a state of grace. Fortunately Uruguayans actually slow down when they see you set foot in a crosswalk. In Buenos Aires we would have been run over.

We came to a stop in front of a house that had loud music coming out of it.

"They're rehearsing," said Guerra. "Let's wait until they stop because they won't be able to hear us otherwise."

"Let's see, what could we do in the meantime?" I said and slowly cornered her against the door.

She let me come in for the kiss. Waiting for me with her eyes. A long, dizzying kiss. At last, that intimacy. The distance of the secret into the ear. That fusion of two spaces into just one. And through the window of the house a sort of ethno rock was coming, very distorted, with a repetitive, insistent bass, and a woman's voice that shouted: "I had love, I kept it waiting, and when I went back, it wasn't the same, the same." Suddenly they stopped, and we stayed in each other's arms, agitated by that drive inside us, that collision.

"Easy does it," Guerra said, putting her hand on my chest. She said it for both our sakes. She rang the bell. A voice asked:

"Who is it?"

Guerra answered:

"Zitarrosa. I came back from the grave to kick the shit out of you guys."

"Be right there!"

Her friend came to the door. A tiny girl. I wondered if she was the singer. She nodded to me in greeting. The dog darted in like it had been there before. Guerra thanked her friend. Then she asked her if she had a joint or something. Her friend said, "Come in," and Guerra said:

"I'll just be a second."

I was left standing on the sidewalk, and that sudden solitude acted as a mirror. There I was, out of my mind, making out with a twenty-eight-year-old kid in broad daylight, on the street. I pictured my face all red and upset. That would have been another good moment to flee, to disentangle myself from my hormonal agenda. Play the man of mystery, the man with the vanishing act, the invisible man. Dissolve into particles of light. Be everywhere and nowhere. But no. I stayed. I sat down, surrendered to my South American destiny, there on the doorstep watching motorcycles, cars, and people pass. Guerra came back and said:

"Want to come with me, Pereyra? I have to pick something up."

I didn't say anything, but I jumped right up, because yes of course I was going with her. Guerra had dropped off the pit bull but now had me as her lapdog, thrilled to follow her wherever she went.

She told me that immediately after she confronted her boyfriend, she'd gone to stay at the place where we'd just left Mr. Cuco. That had lasted two days, then she'd had to leave because the rehearsals were driving her insane. It was an all-female band called The Pink Date: La Cita Rosa.

"They're good, but if you aren't part of the noise, it kind of gets to you."

"That cover didn't sound that great," I told her.

"Not that version, no," said Guerra. "Some of their other ones are better. They always perform in that angry way, though. I feel like they should calm down a little."

"Where are we going, Guerra?"

"To the end of the rainbow, in search of a treasure," she said, and she took out the joint her friend had given her.

As always, I coughed like an amateur on my first couple of puffs. It burned my lungs. Guerra asked me if I was okay, and I nodded with tears in my eyes. They had recently legalized marijuana consumption in Uruguay. It surprised me that you could smoke on the street like that, without a care in the world. We went up to the avenue and into a shopping arcade. She led me into a place that sold old magazines. I thought the whiskey and the pot must have disoriented her a little bit.

"If I don't find it, they'll kill me," she was saying.

"If you don't find what?"

I fell in with her Candombe step. She was looking for some magazines. The owner let us browse around. There were stacks and stacks of a magazine called *Sports Stars*.

"Look for any issue that has a Black player on the cover wearing a Peñarol jersey."

"What does the Peñarol jersey look like?"

"How can you not know that? It's black and yellow. Try the ones from the sixties."

I looked through magazines that were half coming apart. Faces and faces of players with little mustaches, gelled hair, notaries dressed up as soccer players, posing in their trim little shorts, frolicking after a goal, kicking the ball, leaping into the air. It was like going through a time tunnel. Players before professional soccer and the gym, before advertising and PlayStations, some with a bit of a belly on them, one with a handkerchief fixed to his head with four knots. They looked like my grandpa, Ángel Pereyra, during his time as a diplomat in Portugal. That's when they were around. I could practically hear the nasal-voiced announcers narrating the games on the radio.

Time on that side of the River Plate was different, not so much chronological as total, I thought. In Uruguay all times cohabitate. The owner of the store seemed like he'd been sitting in his chair there since 1967.

Suddenly I stopped in front of a photo of a kind of mixed-looking guy, sitting on the grass on the field, surrounded by soccer balls. I remembered my assignment.

"I've got one here, but he's not all that Black," I said to Guerra, showing her the magazine.

"Spencer! You genius," she said and planted a kiss on me. "Now we just have to find Joya. Also Black."

The Radisson was slowly drifting off into the distance, getting smaller and smaller, like a ship. Guerra told me that in the production part of the movie she was working on she'd been asked to look for magazines that featured Joya and Spencer. That was what the movie was going to be called: *Joya and Spencer.* One of them had been Peruvian and the other Ecuadorian. Guerra started singing, "Joya and Spencer, hand-in-hand with each other. They get into heaven, the two of them brothers." She was dancing slightly. I danced a little for her, almost dancing more on the inside. But apparently this inward dance was not altogether invisible. The owner kept glancing at us out of the corner of his eye, looking uncomfortable, coughing to let us know he was still there. He wasn't too impressed with our intoxicated whirlwind through the dusty peace of his store. "When it came to the game both were great, never better. One would run with the ball, the other handled the headers." Guerra sang moving her butt around with antidepressant impudence.

"How come you don't have any Black people in Buenos Aires?" she asked when she had calmed down.

"We do have Black people. The thing is . . . there are all kinds of different theories, Guerra, but I really need to pee."

"Then pee!"

"Where?" I asked. (I sounded like a little kid).

"Señor, where might we be able to access a bathroom?" she asked over her shoulder.

"There are restrooms at the back of the arcade," said the guy, without raising his gaze from whatever he was doing.

I went all the way to the very back, past the last stores. As I went I saw the tattoo parlor, saw it for a second, passing by, out of the corner of my eye, but from then on it kept flashing in my brain. I went carefully down the spiral staircase, which twisted around into darkness. Perhaps it struck me as so endless because of my somewhat fragile state. It went down like a corkscrew into the Earth's core. That bathroom was a catacomb. I don't know how many things I pondered during my long, drunken piss, one hand pressed against the tiles. The marijuana was weaving rapid theories that seemed brilliant to me and that also, when I tried to hold on to them so I could remember them later, kept unraveling into thin air. Something about Black people in Buenos Aires; it seemed like I understood everything, in a kind of nontransferable clairvoyance. The light, which to save energy was on a timer calculated to serve customers more expeditious than I, suddenly went out.

Now I'm trapped inside that Tuesday like in the movie *Groundhog Day*, I go over it again and again, study it, blow it up in my mind, enlarging each individual moment. I try not to put in anything that didn't happen, but nonetheless I do add angles, takes, perspectives that in that moment I didn't see, because I passed by like we always pass through our lives, as fast as we can, stumbling. And now, obsessed, I learn by heart the songs I heard that afternoon, snippet by snippet, and I look for bigger images of the bills I paid with, look at them as though I were going to have to counterfeit them, I see that the front of the thousand-peso bill in Uruguay shows a palm tree, the Palm Tree of poet Juana de Ibarbourou, planted on the promenade in the neighborhood of Pocitos, near the last house where she lived, I look at the illustrated palm tree, go inside that landscape in ink, look up the palm tree on Google Street View, look under the microscope at the places, the things I saw, the minutes of those hours like a dead man permitted to remember just one day. And there I was in the darkness, releasing my sonorous stream in that bathroom, feeling like I was floating, in my relief, understanding everything, although I know it only felt like I understood. But it doesn't matter. My head was spinning and something in my theory had to do with revolution.

The first spark had been when Guerra was dancing upstairs, and I danced, too, albeit on a tiny scale, making a slow little turn to the left. I thought about that. And how she liked it when I did it. I remembered something I'd read at some point: some anthropologists once did a study of dance and movement. They specifically measured the reactions and decisions of women presented with men they'd have to choose between after seeing them dance. One of their conclusions stated that women, in all cultures, preferred men who rotated more on their left leg than on their right. Turning to the left is more seductive than turning to the right. But why? As if there were some cellular behavior, from when we were the size of bacteria, when the whole gamut of options for movement was whether to turn one way or the other. I had made that rotation, I had made Guerra laugh, then I went to the bathroom, and the staircase turned to the left. I went down the spiral, my spiral. Your spiral, Cata, the IUD. To have or not to have a son. Or a daughter. I thought about a daughter, I think for the first time in my life. A daughter! I could have had a daughter. I thought about matryoshka dolls, a woman inside a woman inside a woman, I thought about the chain of orgasms that has brought us to today, in my case a succession of Spanish boys and girls and Portuguese boys and girls getting it on, and some Irish couples on my mother's side whispering sweet, sexy nothings into each other's ears, inseminating each other and devouring each other's hearts. Where did my spiral come from, and where was it going? What was that Afro bass there, that pulse that Guerra had unwound in her mini Candombe and that had continued resounding in me? The Black men's Peñarol. That low drum that grounds the rest, almost guttural, that dance as if the sand under your feet were burning you. Was the animal that I was not going to have more kids? Had its reproductive mission finished? I was in the exact middle of my life, up until then I had been just getting started, but this was the boundary line, the end of the rainbow, as far as the rope could go down, now all that remained was to return, to travel the staircase in the other direction, untwisting myself. My destiny, for some reason, had been to push down on the cold button on the toilet in that basement in Montevideo, a secret button that activated some imperceptible mechanism of the machine, which absorbed the black whirlpool, the roar of the lion in the bathroom I feared so much as a child . . . I was, in that moment, just a drunk man peeing, it is true, and I was stoned, but I was in raptures over my big personal night, my stars like dragons in the sky, comets caught in the vortex, the rotation of the Earth, the possibility of seeing in the total darkness through the window of an instant the infinite spectacle of the Cosmos. I shook off the last drops, fastened my pants and groped my way toward the exit until I could find the light sensor again.

I climbed slowly and, half blinded by the neon lights, went inside the tattoo parlor. A bald guy with a goatee greeted me. He'd had to stop doing whatever had been occupying his attention on the computer.

"How much would it be to get a tattoo in one color on my shoulder, here?"

"Depends on the complexity of it," he said.

"Something simple . . ."

"Oh, probably fifteen hundred pesos, more or less."

"And how long would you take to do it?"

"Could be half an hour, an hour. Like I say, depends on the complexity."

I asked to see symbols for war: guerra. I thought I would get a tattoo of a secret ideogram on my shoulder. He showed me some Chinese ideograms in some laminated folders, but none of them was right. The Celtic symbols were more my style. There were a lot of them, some intricate and intertwined like medieval illuminations, others simpler. When I saw the triskele, I thought: that's the one. The three connected spirals. It made perfect sense with my subterranean intuitions, as if I had come up to seek out that specific image knowing it would be there.

The tattoo cost me twelve hundred pesos (one Juana de Ibarbourou and one Figari wearing big round glasses with an angry expression on his face). About forty dollars.

"Left or right shoulder?"

"Left."

He printed it out and stuck it on me with a washable ink to see how it looked. I looked at my shoulder in the mirror. It looked good. He asked me to take off my T-shirt. Guerra came in looking for me. When she saw me sitting inside the tattoo parlor, she started laughing.

"I can't leave you alone for one minute, Pereyra," she said.

"I'm going to get a tattoo of a heart that says 'Guerra' in the middle," I said.

"No! Don't let him," she said to the tattoo artist. "He's wasted."

"Or maybe I'll get 'Sweetness in the Distance.'"

Guerra stepped up, looked at my shoulder and saw the triskele design.

"That's lovely!" she said.

"You thought I was going to get your name tattooed? With you what I need is a tattoo that will help me forget, not remember: an anti-tattoo. What kind of tattoos do you have for people who want to get a woman off their minds?" I asked the tattoo artist.

The guy smiled as he kept working and didn't respond. It didn't hurt that much, it was like a bunch of tiny, quick injections. Suddenly Guerra grabbed on to the elastic of my cash belt, which, now that I wasn't wearing a shirt, she could see sticking out of my pants.

"What is this?" she said, stretching it and then releasing it so it hit me in the back.

"Fft!" I said. "That's my sports bra."

I tried to hide the elastic inside my boxer shorts. But the tattoo artist asked me not to move so much, and I remained in that position that gave away my crude smuggling trick.

My cell phone vibrated. I thought it was the warning that my battery was running low again, but no. It was your message: *Who is Guerra?* Fuck. The first thing I thought was: How does she know? It seemed impossible to me. Because I was stoned, I thought it must have been something like skin telepathy, like my skin had communicated with yours, and you'd felt something that had set off some kind of alarm in you. Total ridiculousness. Guerra saw my face.

"You okay?"

"Yes."

"Does it hurt?"

"No."

"How long does it take?" she asked the tattoo artist.

"Twenty minutes," he told her.

She went out to talk on the phone in the passageway of the arcade. I realized that you had seen Guerra's email. But you didn't know if Guerra was a man or a woman, because her email address was just initials and a number, and in the messages themselves I called her Guerra, and she didn't sign a name, or if she did, it was only with the letter *M.* I thought. I wasn't sure. Just in case, I answered you as neutrally as possible. *One of the people who invited me to Valizas last year.* I didn't say if it was a man or a woman. It was very telltale, but it was what came to me in the moment while I was buying time and considering what I was going to tell you. My message sent, and my phone turned off, definitively out of battery.

What a disaster, I thought. You had heard me say Guerra in my sleep more than once. What was I going to tell you? That I was repeating the name of some Uruguayan man named Guerra? That I was in love with a Juan Luis Guerra or a Maximiliano Guerra? How was I going to get out of this? I thought maybe I could leave it as a mystery to me, too. Who knew why I'd been repeating that word in my sleep? It was still suspicious: your wife hears what she thinks is "war," "guerra," in the night, and then she finds out that you're going to meet up with a person whose name is Guerra. Of course it made you wonder. On top of which, the email said, *Same place as last time.* It could have been a second meeting with one of the organizers. I had to come up with something I could tell you that would not be too contradictory.

The tattoo was starting to hurt. Not the needle, but the cloth the guy had run over my shoulder to get rid of the excess ink. I thought about my laptop. It would have been hard for you to get in. Maybe you had seen the email on the tablet. I remembered that the day before Maiko had insisted on watching cartoons while I was responding to something on the tablet, and I'd put on YouTube for him, perhaps without closing my email. That could have been it. You always came back early on Tuesdays. Maybe you picked it up and sat down in the armchair in the living room to take a look at your favorites on Pinterest, something like that, you wanted to check your email, and there was my Gmail open on the tablet. What a dumbass. You're a dumbass, too, though, for reading my private correspondence.

Guerra was pacing back and forth in front of the tattoo parlor with her phone to her ear. She looked like she was on edge. She was gesticulating with her other hand. She was upset with someone. Could she be having an argument with her father? Her ex-boyfriend? Then I saw her get more still, barely talking into the phone; her eyes were red. She looked like she was listening. She was shaking her head. I asked the tattoo artist if he was almost done. He said he was, he just had to fill in what he'd outlined a little, and we'd be through.

"Boy, the vibe really changed, didn't it?" the guy said a moment later. "You guys were laughing your heads off, and now it's like a funeral."

"It's fine," I said. "Everything's fine."

When he finished, he cleaned it off and covered the tattoo with a square of plastic wrap and an adhesive cloth. He gave me some tips on skincare for the first few days. I put on my T-shirt, I paid him, and I left.

EIGHT

Out of the arcade, Guerra told me that she was fine, that nothing was wrong, that she'd been upset with the director of production. I didn't know whether to believe her.

"What about the magazines?"

"That old man was robbing people. I put them at the bottom of the stack so later, if they actually give me the money, I'll go back for them. At least I know they're there now."

She wanted to see how my tattoo looked. I showed her. We looked at each other without knowing what to say. Guerra's face then was the saddest face I'd ever seen.

"You're not okay, Guerrita. Come on, let's go."

I put my arm around her shoulder, and we walked. The avenue I'd walked down so enthusiastically that morning was now a different avenue, more rushed, no sun, grayer, less friendly. For a little while we didn't talk. Then Guerra said, "You're good for me." And snuggled up to my side.

Where were we going? We went inside a little store and started grabbing things. We were coming down off the pot, and our bodies wanted sugar. Guerra went to the back and returned with something in her hand.

"Now you'll see what good is, Argentine," she said and showed me a package of alfajores that had a girl wearing a kerchief on the wrapper who resembled her a bit. I took some hard candies, some suckers, and chocolate.

We went along the street, opening them and consuming them with passion and devotion. Guerra was smiling again.

"They ought to open a store called Comedown Seeks Snack," I said.

"Great idea."

"It would be a stoner's paradise. With desserts you can turbocharge, like at ice cream places. A jar of dulce de leche with M&M's. Chocolate with fruit chews . . ."

"A lollipop with a chocolate center," she suggested.

"Genius, that has not been invented yet."

"But I'd call the place Sugar, in English so it would sound cool." We kept talking about this project for several blocks. Suddenly in the window of a music store a ukulele hypnotized me. I stopped dead. It was adorable, like a tiny guitar.

"What?" she said.

"I need to buy that for my kid," I said, thinking aloud, pointing to the ukulele. Still standing there like I was paralyzed.

"So get it," Guerra said.

We went in. The salesman approached us. A bald guy with a goatee that looked very familiar. It was the tattoo artist.

"Didn't you just do my tattoo?" I asked in surprise, and I said to Guerra, "Isn't he the guy who did my tattoo?"

"He is!" cried Guerra.

"Over at Dermis, in the shopping arcade?" he asked.

"Yes . . ."

"That's my brother."

"That's your brother?" asked Guerra.

"Twin brother," he nodded.

We celebrated the coincidence. What are the odds that a person would get a tattoo from one guy and then, without having any idea, go directly to the store several blocks away where his twin is selling musical instruments? It depends on the distance, the size of the city, the options it offers, the connection between the two employees . . . Maybe music and tattoos belong to the same universe, and in that case, the coincidence was not all that strange. I showed him my tattoo; it had gone down a little, and there were a few droplets of blood under the plastic wrap. The guy was somewhere between happy and sick of discussing his twin. I asked him to see the ukulele, and then I tried it out. It sounded good. It came with a booklet of basic chords and ways to tune it. It cost me a hundred and fifty dollars. I took it and carried it in my hand, without a bag or a box. Evidently the money was burning a hole in my pocket. The hotel, lunch, the tattoo, the ukulele . . . I had managed to spend more than five hundred dollars in a day.

"Where are we going?" I asked Guerra on the sidewalk, trying to coax a little sound out of the chords.

"We're going to finish this at the Ramírez," she said, showing me the half of the joint that was left. "Do you have time?"

"What's the Ramírez, a plaza?"

"No. The beach, right here."

"What time is it? My phone died."

"Five o'clock," she said.

"I have a little while still. I have to meet a friend at six."

"You got tired of me, Pereyra, you couldn't get me to go to the hotel, so you're leaving."

"Exactly. This Uruguayan woman is the absolute worst . . . No, really, I'm meeting a guy who used to be my teacher. Enzo Arredondo."

"Does he write for *El País*?"

"I think so, or for *El Observador*. A culture section somewhere, I don't remember where."

"I think I know who he is. So what is he a teacher of?"

"He's more of a guru than a teacher. He taught a very atypical workshop in the Almagro neighborhood of Buenos Aires in the nineties, and I went to it for a while. You could do whatever you liked except write with your words. He'd have you record snippets from the radio and edit them, make trailers for old movies, put together poems out of newspaper headlines, record sounds or conversations on the street, take pictures of very specific things: shoes, backs, clouds, trees, protests, cyclists, the people on your block."

"And you couldn't write?"

"Not a text with your own words. You could put together stories with pictures. Do interviews around the neighborhood asking things like: Has any part of your body ever been in a cast? If you could travel anywhere in the world, where would you go? And you would ask the cashier at the supermarket, the guy at the vegetable stand, everybody. He taught you to look and listen. He'd have you go see a tarot reader, or go to an Evangelical church, ufology conventions. He'd have you interview people . . ."

"What a strange old man."

"He's not that old, you know. He's probably around seventy now. Do you want to come with me to meet him?"

"I can't, I have a production meeting in Pocitos later."

"Where does your dad live, Guerra?"

"Around there."

"In Pocitos?"

"Yes."

"You're a ritzy rich girl from Pocitos?"

"What are you talking about? Stop, I'm no ritzy anything."

"You just act like you're workin' for a living, bus boy, bartender . . ."

"I'm middle class, as my mom used to say, 'with aspirations.' The only ritzy person here is you."

"Yeah, but at least I admit it. You'll see when you're forty-five what a little lady you'll become. I've got your number now."

"Maybe so," she said, slightly offended, and lit what was left.

This time I didn't cough. In one hand I had the ukulele and the alfajor, in the other the joint.

"This alfajor is glorious."

"You see? Salty! From the sierras in Minas."

"But it's not salty, it's sweet . . ."

"No, in Montevideo we say salty when . . ."

"I know, I'm just kidding you."

"We seem to have swallowed a clown, I see," said Guerra in a smarmy schoolmarm's tone.

We burst out laughing. She told me that one of her teachers at the "lyceum" used to say that whenever any of the students got up to anything.

I was having a good time with Guerra, I didn't want the afternoon to end. I was getting overheated with my jacket and my backpack on.

"Where is this beach, sugarcane? Valizas? Tennessee? I don't know if I can make it."

"We just have to turn here onto Acevedo, and then we go down and there it is."

"What's this neighborhood called?"

"Cordón."

We went around an older building and turned. Now I know it was the Universidad de la República, which is to say that for a moment we were walking inside their five-hundred-peso bill, which features that building in blue ink. The trees got enormous, gigantic banana trees. The block made its airspace felt, like a cathedral's tall gleaming. We went down toward the promenade. You could see the beach the whole way down. I took a better look at the street sign and remembered:

"Onetti wrote an incredible scene that takes place here. I think it's here. This guy has his wife walk in a white dress. He gets her out of bed at night and brings her here just to have her walk down this street while he watches from over there on the promenade."

Guerra was looking at me like her interest was piqued. I went on:

"He'd seen her when she was young one day walking toward him, and he describes her, you know, gorgeous, with the wind in her dress. And years later he drags her out of bed and makes her come back to the same place to walk in the same way, back and forth, time and again, like he's trying to get back her youth. But it isn't there anymore, now she has this sour expression, this embittered face—she's just not a young girl anymore. 'Nothing could be done and we went back,' the paragraph ends. That son of a bitch. She isn't Caro anymore, now she's Carolina."

"La Ceci," Guerra corrected me. "Cecilia Huerta de Linacero."

"Oh, so you were letting me expound for no reason. You like Onetti?"

"I especially like that book, *The Pit.*"

"I wouldn't have pegged you as an Onetti fan. You're full of surprises."

"Yeah. I think you underestimate me, Pereyra."

"Maybe you're right. But I'm getting to know you. If you think about it, we haven't seen each other very many times. When I saw you today it was almost shocking. After thinking about you so much it was like I had invented you, inside myself."

"You thought I was ugly?"

"No, the opposite, so sexy and gorgeous, but just, like, out of sync with my memory. Too real, too liberated from any intervention from me. All those months I had you in my head and could rewind you, fast-forward you, pause you. I'd open and close the emails you'd send me. You know how you can go over things in your memory, relive them . . . And when you came today it was like you super-imposed yourself over the memory I had of you, you just elbowed it right out of the way."

"Sounds a little awful."

"Not at all. It was fascinating. Seriously. And then the whiskey put it all together. You became a unified, single being again. It was just a matter of listening to you and looking at you. That's what I mean about getting to know you. I like it."

"What?"

"Getting to know you."

"You're quite the seducer, Pereyra. It's really remarkable. Your mind comes up with all these little pirouettes."

I felt all the wind off the ocean at once. I saw into the distance.

"Why do they call this the river, when it's the ocean?"

"It's a mix," she said. "The ocean really begins in Punta del Este, that's what they say. But here there are some days when it's greener, or bluer, with saltwater, and then there are some days when it's just brown, and that means it's mostly river here."

Before going down to the beach, we leaned back against the railing. Behind the breakwater there were some guys kitesurfing, with colorful sails that swayed and meandered like paragliders.

"Guerra, I need to tell you something."

"What?"

"I don't want to be your gay friend." I looked at her. "Don't laugh, dumbass, I'm serious. I don't want to be a buddy you can dance around with without having to think about the consequences. The helpful advisor, the sympathetic ear that's always ready to listen. I want to be good for you, but that's not all I want. I'm not some teddy bear."

"Dude, get a grip. First of all, my gay friends give the worst advice of anyone I know. If I followed their advice I'd be fucking seven different guys at once. My gay friends are not even remotely interested in my sniveling. And secondly . . . secondly . . . I don't remember what the second thing was because this joint is actually pretty strong."

I kissed her, and as we kissed, she ran her hand over the back of my neck, and it sent an electric charge all the way down my back. She reset me. I forgot everything, my name. We held each other, and when I opened my eyes I saw something weird in the sky. At first I thought it was one of the paragliders, but it was bigger than that.

"Look at that!"

It was like an enormous diamond shape that looked like it was vibrating, or glimmering, high above the surface out at sea.

"What is that?"

"The waiter from the place where we had lunch told me they saw something like this yesterday. I didn't take it seriously, though."

"What is that, Lucas? I'm scared. What could it be?"

It was darker in the middle and pinker around its edges, which seemed to undulate. It had a bit of a butterfly feel to it. Then suddenly it was gone. We tried to find it again, all up and down the horizon, but it didn't come back. We couldn't believe what we'd seen.

"Do you think we hallucinated it?" Guerra said. A guy was coming toward us quickly wearing jogging gear, and I asked him:

"Did you just see a pinkish light, like a diamond in the sky?"

The guy stopped, and I had to repeat the question because he had his headphones in.

"Yeah, I saw it. It has to be some meteorological phenomenon, that's what I'm assuming. Or the U.S. is conducting some experiment. They're always somewhere with their navy ships, doing strange things," he said and resumed his exercise.

We went down to the beach and walked along the shore without our sneakers on. Or rather, as Guerra would have put it: we walked along the shore without our "Nikes" on. Guerra was saying that maybe what we'd seen was like a forcefield or a portal that opens and closes.

"But who generates it? What's it for?"

"It self-generates. It's energy."

"But what happens through that portal?"

"How would I know? I have no idea."

"You know what it looked like? You're going to think I'm really sick . . ."

"Yeah . . ."

"A cunt!" I said.

"Yes! Such a cunt!" shouted Guerra.

"The cunt of God!" I shouted.

We fell onto the sand. We were a couple of potheads prowling around in the world. The astonishing, incomprehensible world. There was almost no one on the beach. Every now and then someone with a dog. A kid in the distance digging a pit. The wind was blowing, and I started to get cold. We went to sit up against the wall.

There in its shelter we were fine. Guerra was sucking on a lollipop. I tried to get "Zamba For You" out of the ukulele, the Zitarrosa song the girls from La Cita Rosa had mangled, but I didn't know the chords, and my knowledge of the guitar confused me more than helped. Now I can play it without any flubs, plucking and everything, and every time I sing it I'm right there by her side, impressing her with my rendition: "I'm not singing to you: what sings to you is zamba."

But at the time my efforts didn't sound very good. I was more interested in Guerra focused on her sucker. I got out mine. Hers was purple, and mine was red. The kind of sucker that's a little ball. We started discussing them: "Is that one grape?" "Let me see that." "Let me see yours." We swapped lollipops. And then a kiss that tasted like strawberry, a kiss that tasted like grape. More kisses, many sweet kisses, sheltered by the wall that created a little nook up against a set of stone steps. We ended up on our sides in the sand. You'll be the death of me, Guerra. We always end up in the sand. I write it like this because there weren't any orderly dialogues, one after the next, but rather words breathed into each other's ears, with no space in between them. A single whispered breath. She touched my cock through my pants. She pulled down my zipper. She stuck her hand in and took hold of my cock. "Well, well, you're no stuffed animal, Pereyra, that's for sure—I never had a stuffed animal with something like this." We covered ourselves a little with my jacket, but we also didn't care.

We were off. I kissed her neck, I held her breasts under her T-shirt and her much-discussed sports bra. "Guerra, let's go to Brazil together. Let's take the bus tonight. Let's go for a week." She didn't say anything, she just kept jerking me off. "We could be by ourselves in Brazil by tomorrow afternoon. I'll take care of everything." "Shh," she said. "Let's go," I said. She didn't say anything. I felt her face get wet. I saw a couple of tears on her cheeks. She was barely shaking her head. She unbuttoned my pants. "Baby, Guerra, I want to fuck you so bad, I want to be inside you so bad. I can't stop saying your name. Sometimes I say it in my sleep." Guerra was crying silently. She was looking into my eyes. She was holding me tightly, opening her mouth between gasps. "Let's go to Brazil today." I felt her have a spasm of sadness, crying, but she didn't stop jerking me off. She confessed into my ear: "I'm pregnant, too, Lucas." I looked at her. She nodded. "Two months, I don't know if I'm going to have it." I held her close to me. "Exercise caution when getting in the water when there is no lifeguard present," said an old sign on the wall. Recalculating. No one is just one person, each of us is a hub of people, and Guerra's hub was among the more complicated ones. "I want you to come." The lights in my brain flickered yellow. I didn't know what was happening, but I was still hard. I didn't know what to say. Guerra moved her head toward my cock. She looked at me. "Come," she said. She took her tongue and slid it over the head. That was when I heard the footsteps and felt the kick in my ribs.

NINE

I was facing away from the ocean and the two guys had come from that way. I thought there were two. "Stay still and keep your mouth shut." But I couldn't open my mouth because one of them had smashed my face into the sand, I don't know if it was with his knee or his foot, but he was jamming something into the back of my neck. Pressing down on my back with his whole weight. It all happened so fast. The thing that terrified me the most was having my dick out and my pants undone. My modesty was more powerful than my fear of death. Guerra was saying, "No, no, no!" When I heard that they were shaking her, I tried to get up, and they started kicking me again, this time in my stomach. In the grip of that pain, I was sidelined. All that existed was that godawful suddenness. There was a silence. And they ran off. I couldn't breathe. When I finally did breathe again, I had sand in my mouth, and I almost choked on it. I spit and sucked in sand. Guerra was asking me if I was okay. I couldn't answer. I was slowly getting my breath back. I opened my eyes. She was fine. I touched my side, where they had kicked me the first time. It hurt. I touched my stomach. The money belt was gone. My backpack was gone, too.

"Which way did they go?" I asked Guerra, buttoning up my pants.

"That way, up the stairs," she said. "But wait, Lucas, stay here."

I went up the stairs. Guerra behind me. I started running, randomly, wherever, I didn't care. I ran across the street and almost got run over. A car slammed on its brakes, and then I was on top of the hood. I got off and kept running. Guerra, standing on the promenade, shouting.

"Lucas, wait!"

But Lucas couldn't wait because Lucas had just been jumped and had lost fifteen grand in dollars. Two hundred and twenty-five grand in Argentine pesos, four hundred and fifty grand in Uruguayan pesos. The biggest dumbass in all of the Americas. I couldn't not run a little, at least. At least to flee the black clouds amassing over my head, my perfect storm, my personal mafia that had just won the battle, and I was running along the sidewalk on the other side of the promenade shouting "You motherfuckers, you motherfuckers." People stared.

Suddenly you're the crazy person in those situations, the man out of control. I stopped short and looked in all directions. Cars drove by, indifferent to my personal microdrama, my desperation. I crossed the street a few times without knowing what direction to go in, I got stuck on the little island between the two lanes, lost, gasping, furious as the Incredible Hulk in the middle of that avenue. I kept thinking this couldn't really be happening, and I would check my groin, the absence of the cash that had been there three minutes before. "No way, no way," I said in all possible tones, from tearful supplication to scream of incomprehensible fury. I jogged back to where Guerra was standing with the ukulele in her hand.

"Lucas, calm down, you're going to get run over. You almost got run over. Please, calm down."

"Are you okay? Did they hit you?"

"No," said Guerra. "They knocked me down when I tried to stand up, but they didn't hurt me."

"Two guys?"

"Yeah."

"What did they look like?"

"I don't know, like two guys. I didn't get a good look because I was scared. They were wearing gym clothes, I think. I think they left on a motorcycle because I heard one starting when they went up. Did they get a lot of money?"

I nodded. I was so ashamed. Infinitely ashamed. And suddenly I was enraged. I grabbed the ukulele. I raised my arm to smash it against the railing of the promenade, and Guerra seized my wrist, on tiptoes.

"Don't break it," she said and didn't release me.

Wise words. Not only because it was a gift for Maiko, or because after, in the months that followed, that tiny instrument kind of saved my life, but also because destroying it there on the promenade would have served only to underscore my own stupidity with a ridiculous act. The image of me shattering the ukulele against a column like a shrunken Jimi Hendrix . . . The scale was ridiculous, a mini-gaucho Martín Fierro shattering his guitar, you'd have to change the stanza slightly: "At this point, the singer/reached for a bottle to comfort him,/he took a drink deep as the sky/and brought his story to an end/and with one blow, smashed his guitar/into splinters on the floor."

I was left with what I had on, the ukulele in my hand, and a little bit of Uruguayan money in my pocket. With my backpack they had taken my phone, my house keys, my car keys, my wallet with my credit cards . . . My passport had been spared because as soon as they'd given me the money in the bank I'd put it in the inside pocket of my jacket. I clutched my head and walked. The fear and the adrenaline had eliminated from my bloodstream the floating feeling I'd had from the alcohol and the pot. I was sober, and there was a sort of high-pitched feedback that was deafening me. Guerra was talking to me, trying to calm me down. I couldn't listen anymore. I was trying to figure out if there was any solution, but was irreparable. Those two guys would be in some distant neighborhood of Montevideo by now, on their motorcycle, counting up my money. Regardless I got it in my head that I had to report it to the police, and I asked Guerra where there was a station. Suddenly I was like a German tourist; I couldn't even interact with people. Guerra asked where the police station was and took me up along the edge of Rodó Park until we went up Salterain Street.

What so recently had worried me—your question about who Guerra was, the story I was going to have to make up, the other emails that you might have seen and that I wasn't sure if I'd deleted—all that had faded into the background. Now the problem was the money that wasn't there anymore. How was I going to explain coming back empty-handed? What could I possibly come up with to justify such extreme stupidity? How had I let myself get robbed that easily? Why had I put myself in such a vulnerable position? Guerra gave me a glance every so often.

"I'm sorry to put you through all this, Guerrita. I honestly never thought something like this could happen to me."

"Don't worry about me."

"We were on another planet, weren't we?"

"Yes," she said. "A very pleasant planet."

"And you're pregnant," I remembered. "Are you sure they didn't hit you?"

"I'm sure. Does it hurt where they kicked you?" she asked me. "I don't know how you can walk."

"My side hurts, here."

Guerra lifted up my shirt, the skin was red, but nothing like the bruise that came afterward, like a cloud of purple, blue, and in the end, kind of green. On my belly I had a scrape from the money belt, from when they ripped it off me.

"We should take you to the hospital so they can check that out."

"I'm okay," I said.

"What are you going to do?"

"About what?"

"Tonight, Lucas, what are you going to do, are you going back?"

"Yeah, I guess so, I have my passport. I can go back."

"Do you want me to lend you money so you can take a taxi?"

"No need. I have some money in my pocket."

When we got to the corner where the police station was, Guerra asked me if I could report the theft on my own because she had to get to her meeting.

"Go, I'll be fine."

"If anything comes up just go to an internet café and send me an email, or get a phone card. I'll send you an email with my number and the number at my dad's place right now. If you want to stay there tonight, you're more than welcome."

"Thank you."

We hugged, exchanged the quickest peck like faces bouncing off each other, and I watched her walk away.

She turned around and blew me a kiss. The most beautiful thief in the world. That's what I thought when I started walking again, I wondered if maybe she hadn't wanted to go into the police station with me. Was that possible? I walked. Was that really possible? Had that been her plan? I looked over my shoulder: Guerra was gone.

On my last trip I'd told her I'd be back to take out money. She knew. "Were you able to take care of your errands?" she had asked me that afternoon, almost as soon as we met up. Later she saw my money belt when I was getting my tattoo, she had a heated conversation with someone over the phone, she took me to the beach, she undid my pants . . . In just a few steps on the street a thousand images connected in my mind. Was it her boyfriend who had robbed me? Was she acting? Was it all an act? That whole afternoon? Did she cry on the beach because she was betraying me? I thought about that tiny pause, that silence when they kicked me a second time. Had it been Guerra giving them the sign to leave? A sign of "that's enough, don't hit him anymore." Was it Guerra directing the whole thing? Was she the boss of those two guys? I imagined her stopping them with a single tiny gesture, then telling them to scram, with simply a movement of her eyes. The boss.

"How can I help you?" asked the policeman standing in the door.

I looked at him.

"I doubt you can," I said and kept walking.

TEN

I stood there at a corner not knowing which way to go. I have rarely been so lost. I knew where I was but didn't know where I was going. My immediate future was complete confusion. I could go to the Radisson and throw myself out the window on the twentieth floor, although it might have been one of those anti-suicide, anti-smoking windows they seal shut. I could also sleep there until I decided what to do. I could leave that night for Brazil with the money I had in my pocket, flee from everything, from you, from myself, from my son, my house, my inexplicable idiocy, and live my life instead of writing it. Start a new life there, work . . . But what the fuck was I going to do in Brazil? I was in a choose-your-own-adventure moment, and all the adventures I had in mind ended badly. I also didn't understand the recent past, because I didn't know what exactly had happened to me. The possibility that Guerra was to blame brought about a total retrospective uncertainty in me. I was lost in time. All I could do was step on my present, on my shadow, be still there. The rest was vertigo.

I don't know how long I stood in place. Until a ragged-looking guy approached, with his wild mane of hair, his teeth in ruins, his many bags. I didn't see him until he was right in front of me. He said:

"Play one for the papooses."

"I don't know how to play it," I said, looking at the ukulele. "I just got it."

"You'll have to learn. So we can all dance," said the guy and took a few dance steps with his pants half falling off.

I crossed the street, walked down the sidewalk like a deer in headlights. Simple motion was drawing me out of my autism. "You'll have to learn." That was true. I remembered Enzo and went in the direction of his house.

It was on Fernández Crespo, almost at the corner. Closer than I'd realized. I found the door to the street but didn't know what apartment he was. I thought he was on the fifth floor, but I wasn't sure. I looked up. From the sidewalk I shouted:

"Enzo! Enzo!"

A woman appeared.

"It's Lucas!" I said.

A minute later Enzo came to the same window, naked, giving me the salute President Perón used to give from the balcony when he would raise both his open hands over his head like he was giving the dimensions of the enormous fish he caught one time, and he shouted:

"The Dutch! I'll be right down."

He came down in a loose shirt, long pants, and sandals. Slight, with a decisive step, balder than the last time, ears withering, an attitude that was in between relaxed and dangerous, a backwater Yoda. We hugged. By the time we had gotten up to his apartment, I had told him everything.

A woman who must have been around forty opened the door for us. She had light-colored eyes. I didn't recognize her.

"They jumped him," Enzo said.

"You were robbed?" she asked in alarm.

I had to tell the story all over again. In more detail, between offers of coffee, explanations about the ukulele, the offered possibility of calling Buenos Aires. I could have called you on the home phone, Cata, but I didn't know what I was going to tell you yet. Enzo served me coffee in a glass cup. I added some sugar. Was this woman Enzo's daughter, a student, or his new girlfriend?

"That is so strange, because people don't really get robbed like that at the Ramírez," she said.

"They followed him!" Enzo said and turned to me. "They targeted you. They waited until you were in a place where there weren't so many people."

"They followed me the whole afternoon? When I left the bank I went down the street that runs behind the Solís

Theatre, there wasn't anyone around, and I was sitting at the Santa Catalina restaurant for a while, too, with no one around . . . They could have robbed me there."

"They're professionals," said Enzo. "You can't outsmart them."

"I wouldn't have thought that after that much time they'd still be following me."

"Now, tell me . . . what were you doing on your own on the beach with all that cash? Who would dream of doing such a thing?" Enzo scolded me.

I didn't mention Guerra. To protect her, to protect myself. From that moment on I would have been on my own at the beach, sitting in the sand, watching the guys jumping and flying in the waves as they kitesurfed. I could erase Guerra from the whole movie. Me having lunch on my own at the restaurant, on my own on the street, on my own at the shopping arcade, at the music store . . . It could have been the tattoo artist who arranged it, he saw me with the money belt, too, or maybe his brother because I paid for the ukulele in dollars. Even the kid at the Radisson could have done it, or someone from the bank. It could even have been random. I would have had my shirt raised up, partly exposing the money belt, when I was lying in the sand. Or if it was Guerra's boyfriend, he could have followed her, he might be angry with her, he might have gotten revenge by hitting me and taking everything I had. Maybe he'd seen the emails, maybe he knew about me. Why not him?

I sat in silence before my coffee. I started answering everything in monosyllables.

"Do you want to rest for a while?"

"No."

"Do you want to wash up a little? You've got sand on your face."

I went to the bathroom. I did have sand on my face, in my hair. I looked like I'd been in an accident, knocked down by some rough happenstance of fate. I tried to get it off in the sink but couldn't, and I was getting sand everywhere. I opened the door a crack and said:

"Enzo, I'm going to take a quick shower."

"Of course, no problem," he said. "The blue towel is clean."

I got undressed and got under the stream of cold water that gradually warmed up. I thought about Guerra, when she had snuggled up to me and told me that I was good for her, and how I shielded her and protected her with my body while continuing to walk. Now the water was hot. Steam was rising. Suddenly I surprised myself by bursting into tears. It had been a long time since I'd cried. Leaning against the tiles, trying to stifle my whimpers, biting my arm. You cried sitting at the kitchen counter, Maiko cries every day, the stiff-legged lady the Evangelist on the bus helped forgive cried, and both Guerra and her friend who betrayed her cried. We all cry. In tears "that gather downward to the sea / We know as Death," Manrique might say. I never cry, less so out of sadness.

Love makes me cry, tenderness. I cried because I thought of Guerra and realized I was never going to see her again, I refused to believe that her tenderness wasn't real, and I felt your love, too, Catalina, beyond the shadow of a doubt, and the love of my child wrapped around me holding on to my neck when he doesn't want me to leave. And Enzo's hospitality, his blue towel. When someone attacks you, you get more alert, as if you were alone in the world, and when out of nowhere someone treats you nicely, you let your guard down, and you fall apart. Tenderness is what really knocks you down.

I had to go back to Buenos Aires. I knew that.

I dried off and got dressed. I could feel that crying had cleared up my chest, but I noticed that when I breathed deeply, my ribs hurt on the left side.

"I left a sand dune in the bathroom."

"Don't you worry," said Enzo. "Have a seat. Clarita, there's an orange cake in the pantry."

"I'll bring it right out," she said, getting up.

Clara was a beautiful woman, definitely around my age. She seemed relaxed, slightly tousled, with a peace in her voice like she was high on the endorphins of a recent orgasm. Had I interrupted something when I'd shouted from the street? Enzo looked the same way, but Enzo always looked like that. She definitely wasn't his daughter. That was for sure.

When we were alone, he asked me:

"How much money did they get?"

"Fifteen thousand dollars."

"Fuck."

"It was the money I got for two books, columns for *Milenio* and a novel for Astillero."

"In Spain?"

"Yeah. I have to turn them both in in May. With the dollars I was going to have about nine months to work. And I would have paid off my debts. I owe everybody money. I don't know what I'm going to do."

"Have you started the novel?"

"No. I was going to start it now."

Clara came back with the cake. Enzo was still thinking. Finally he said:

"You have to be careful with Montevideo. Montevideo will kill you without a second thought. Every now and then it does, just lays somebody out. Look at Fogwill."

"Fogwill died in Buenos Aires."

"Yeah, but days after coming here, where the cold got him. And what about the one from the *Orsai* magazine, what was his name?"

"Casciari."

"He had a heart attack here in Montevideo, barely lived to tell the tale. There is something like a Bermuda Triangle here, it's not to be underestimated. It's kind of the B-side of the River Plate, the side that'll eat you right up. If you can't handle it, it'll kill you. You have to be careful with Uruguay, especially if you come thinking it's like the countryside in Argentina only everybody's good, there's no corruption, no Peronism, you can smoke pot on the street, the cute little country where everyone is a good person and friendly and all that bullshit. If you're not paying attention, Uruguay will fuck you in the ass."

"Enzo!" said Clara.

"That's how it is, my love, that's how it is. Just think of the Maracanaço on the Brazilians."

Clara went into the kitchen.

"Don't underestimate these Charrúas," Enzo said to me quietly so she wouldn't hear.

He showed me purple marks on his shoulder, which looked like tooth marks.

"They're biters . . ."

Enzo, counting on his fingers, enumerated:

"The rugby players who ate their friends in the accident in the Andes, the Indians who ate Solís, the Suárez shark that bit that Italian, this one," he said pointing to the kitchen. "It's no coincidence. They are not to be underestimated. They took a bite out of you, too."

I stayed silent, eating the cake.

"Although they did you a favor, Dutch. That dough was poisoned, that's why you let them jump you like that. You didn't feel like it belonged to you."

"Don't therapize me."

"I'm not therapizing you, but you've got to see this as a liberation. You were going to have to write a thousand-page tome just to pay off your debt. Nobody should write like that."

"It wasn't a debt, it was time, that money was time to write without having to take another shitty job."

"I would not have read the mess you could have written with all that dough in all those months. Who ever heard of paying for books that haven't been written yet?"

He looked at me and continued:

"I promise you it isn't envy, or maybe it is a little, but books have to be written, that's the first step, and then you decide how much they're worth. As Girondo said, you polish them like diamonds and then you sell them like a string of sausages. You they paid for diamonds, yet you would have twirled a string of sausages at them in return."

"How am I supposed to write with my kid dangling from my balls, reading ten thousand students at once, teaching classes? How the fuck am I supposed to write like that?"

"Write about that."

"About what?"

"About that, what you're telling me, what's happening now in this situation."

"Now's not the time to play the Zen master."

I got up and looked out the open window. You could see far: the roofs, the antennas, the lights of the houses that were starting to gleam. It was getting dark. I looked at his overflowing library. His books were like mine are now, in double rows on the shelves.

"You're going to go back to poetry, Dutch. You're too angry still to know it. The anger will have to pass."

"But what am I going to do? All I have is the five hundred dollars I exchanged into Uruguayan pesos, and I already spent some of that on whiskey. I was supposed to pay off my debts, pay back my wife, the preschool, the insurance, a thousand other things. She's waiting for me to get back with that money so we can patch up all those holes."

"How many pesos do you have left?"

"I don't know. Five thousand, something like that."

"I know it's not great timing, but could you lend me three thousand, and I'll give it back to you in two weeks when I go over there?"

I looked at him with a straight face, and he looked at me with a smile. I burst out laughing. Enzo laughed, too:

"I'll give it back to you with interest in two weeks. My pension comes next week."

I handed him two bills, and he said:

"The world isn't for guys like you and me. That whole thing about dating all the girls, earning all the money, blowing it, owning fancy cars. We can't pull it off. You can't because deep down you don't want to. You'd rather be melancholic just like me. Surplus value makes you uncomfortable."

"Stop lecturing me."

"Done. I'll be quiet." He watched me stand there. "What are you going to do?"

"I'm going to go to the port."

"Do you have enough for the taxi?"

"I think so. If I don't hit any other little tolls . . ."

"I'll give it back to you in Buenos Aires, we'll get a pizza at Pin-Pun. I'll take you out. Now, go back, get some sleep, tell your wife what happened . . ."

"Just in case, please don't tell anyone."

"Never you fear. In Buenos Aires we'll discuss the magazine. It's a guaranteed failure."

I said goodbye to Clara. Enzo walked me downstairs. We said goodbye, and he said:

"Don't get bitter."

Then it was absurd because I had forgotten the ukulele, and after he let me out I had to start tapping the glass on the door, so he opened again, and we went back up and came back down, but without saying a word this time. I'd worn out my farewell. When he opened the door to let me out onto the street, I gave him a couple of slaps on the back and said:

"Good luck with the biter."

ELEVEN

I was among the last to board the ferry. It was a new one, snazzy, baptized *Francisco*, I assumed in honor of the Pope, with carpets so impeccable that before getting on you were required to put gauze coverings over your shoes, the kind they have in operating rooms, so as not to sully anything. Chilean tourists, Uruguayan doctors, old Argentine gadabouts of high-society heritage, ladies wearing strident perfumes, families, all of them in those same light blue sneakers, like Smurfs.

In the very back I found a row of four empty seats. I settled in there, I needed to be still for a while. My side was really hurting. If I'd had my backpack, I could have taken a Tylenol from the pack I always carry in the front pocket. What would the thieves have done with my things? I was going to have to cancel my Visa, get a new license, a new insurance card, subway card, registration . . . I zipped up my jacket because the A/C was hitting me right in the face. I put my hands in my pockets, there was sand there, and I found a piece of candy from that afternoon. I opened it, started chewing on it, it was dulce de leche flavored. Sweetness in the distance. I looked at the wrapper: it said ZABALA and featured the face of a historical man, from the eighteenth century, with a long wig with curls and an imperial mustache. It was none other than the founder of Montevideo, as Wikipedia tells me. Bruno Mauricio de Zabala. Candy under Guerra's mother's maiden name. Guerra Zabala sounded like "guerras a bala": it connoted mayhem, bullets, and, of course, war.

How was I going to tell you all this? What was my version of the story going to be? What did it look like from your perspective? Your husband, whose life you've been paying for almost a year, goes over to Uruguay (on a ticket you bought) to get the money he was finally paid and then returns without a peso, with a tattoo on his shoulder and a ukulele in his hand. *You had one job, motherfucker. It wasn't that hard.* Maybe I wouldn't have to lie that much. The robbery had happened. All I had to do was change its backdrop. I could tell you I had been robbed on my way to the parking lot, that in the morning there had been no spaces in the Buquebus lot, which was true, and I had had to park the car farther away, and when I went to get it coming back . . . In fact, the car would stay there in that lot two blocks from the docks.

This is what happened: I walked up to the car, at night, they put a gun to my head, threw me to the ground, kicked me, and took the money. Someone from Customs must have told them about me. I had gone to Uruguay for the day. It was very likely that I was bringing back dollars. In fact, that version sounded much more realistic than what happened, it was easier to understand. Like in the story "Emma Zunz" by Borges, only the circumstances and the time would be false, but everything else would be true: the robbery, my desperate tone, the humiliation, and the violence.

I stuck to that version. I went over it a few more times, and then, when I needed to distract myself with something, I realized I had nothing to read. My Rimbaud biography had stayed on the bedside table at the Radisson. In the end, I paid for a nice room just to house the Rimbaud biography. Would it end up in the hotel's lost and found? Would I be able to send Enzo to pick it up? I took off my sneakers, raised the armrests, and lay down across the length of several seats. The engines were already on. We were moving. I closed my eyes. I'd left Rimbaud crossing the desert on a stretcher carried by twelve Sudanese porters. He was going back sick, tired, penniless, swindled, robbed by the African kings to whom he'd tried to sell arms. He was crossing a lunar landscape where the Danakil, members of the most beautiful and most fearsome tribe, lay in wait. They could have killed the whole caravan and left the bodies to be devoured by lions. His knee swollen, gigantic. He couldn't walk anymore. The world was about to claim its share. A leg. The adventure was ending, he was trying to get back to France where they would amputate it. The canvas of his litter fluttered in the wind. A room for Rimbaud, a bed with clean sheets for the death throes of the greatest poet of all time. A book on the bedside table. Room 262.

I woke up drenched in sweat as we were coming into the port of Buenos Aires. I felt like I had a fever. People were already crowded near the exit.

When I went down the escalator, I sent the ukulele through the scanner, and on the other side a woman asked me to wait. A man palpated me like he was looking for arms. Very rapidly and almost imperceptibly he touched my crotch where the money belt had been. They were looking for wads of bills. They had me take off my jacket, they felt it to see if it had anything hard in it. They had me lift up my shirt. They even looked inside the ukulele. I thought, You're too late, muchachos. Nothing here, nothing there. They stopped and checked others alongside me.

They couldn't get anything off me because I had nothing. They couldn't rob me. They let me through, and I went out into the darkness of the port thinking about that: no one can rob me now. I was going to walk, straight down Córdoba Avenue, more than thirty blocks, some of them completely dark, all the way to our place on Coronel Díaz, but I was going to do it fearlessly, with no paranoia that anyone was following me. The car was there; I didn't have the keys. It stayed there until you went to get it two weeks later. I didn't have Argentine pesos to take a taxi, either. I crossed the tracks of El Bajo, Madero Avenue, Alem, and I climbed the Córdoba ravine. I was destroyed, beaten, but invincible.

It did not occur to me that they would have to put me in the hospital the following day. The fever made everything denser. I thought: I'm going to die, and that's the way it should be. Without that money, I'm immortal. Because of the pain in my ribs, I was walking with my left arm pressed against my body, in a kind of a zombie's stagger. The zombie with the ukulele. Fortunately I hadn't smashed it on the beach or left it at Enzo's. Maiko brought it the first weekend when he came to the apartment I moved into after we separated, and then he left it behind. So it stayed there. I learned chords, rhythms, how to strum it. Then I worked up the courage to pluck it. It saved me from my crash. That tiny mini-guitar fortified my soul throughout this year I've lived alone. What I knew from guitar let me learn quickly. It's a simple instrument but it can also be complex. The guitar had always been too big for me, the chords had sounded messy, too many notes in that bridge. For an autodidact, for somebody who plays by ear like me, the ukulele is ideal. I realized I'd rather play the ukulele well than keep playing the guitar poorly, and that was like a new personal philosophy. If you can't handle life, try a lifelet. Everything had gotten too complicated for me. That whole life we had created together, Cata—it was too big for me. I wasn't well. You weren't, either. We hated each other with our to-do lists. Now I have a chalkboard in the kitchen and I make my lists of pending tasks, but they don't torment me. Your lists tortured me. And I imagine my invisible lists were torture for you, too. My tacit lists, my fickle demands. I assimilated from you those visible lists, and I organize myself pretty well, I would say. Because they're my own lists. I no longer view those tasks as someone else's.

I couldn't walk very fast. I continued down Córdoba, passed the whorehouses with mysterious curtains, the Galerías Pacífico where six years ago I had bought you that Bahía dress that looked so pretty on you when your belly got big. I crossed the 9 de Julio and as always I wished I could get on a ferry that would take me over to the other side. I don't know exactly when they demolished the block that was there in order to make the enormous avenue, but ever since there's been an emptiness, an anti-matter, still palpable today. Today it's a space that is so much more than a block. It's a nothingness you have to cross, and it exhausts even the bravest among us. I kept going, past Plaza Lavalle, the Cervantes Theater, ugly blocks, cold, with no personal references, up to the internet café just before Callao where I would make my photocopies for my classes at the university. The McDonald's, the entrance to the subway. I thought about going down and jumping the turnstile. I felt pretty bad. Everything seemed impossible to me. Except to keep walking, falling forward with every step, like Herzog says when he tells the story of his journey on foot from Munich to Paris.

Would I have been considering it as I traversed those streets? Did I already have the drive to separate from you? What about you? Had you thought about it over the course of that long day when you saw my email and suspected something? We needed a push. That slight force that would let everything that was already fissured crack all the way apart. Was it falling apart because of age? I don't know. What I do know is that we had to stop. Quit gathering spite. Those mornings, for example, those Saturdays or Sundays when Maiko would wake up at seven and want his Nesquik and you and I would start the contest of who could pretend to be most asleep. Maiko would insist, and one of us would get up with hatred, make him the Nesquik, along with coffee for the other one, the lazy one who was pretending to be paralyzed, the one who hadn't slept enough, the one who just can't, who needs more sleep, who's suffering, poor thing, that fucking son of a piece-of-shit bitch. Maiko in the kitchen now with his labor union tactics, moving furniture, chairs, climbing onto the counter, grabbing knives, you have to be there, you have to watch him, you have to take care of the drunken dwarf from dawn on, while the other nestles into those warm sheets, while the other self-cancels, pretends not to exist, but they're there, pretending not to know, in their great betrayal. Then, you or I, the one who had gotten up, would wash the dishes from the night before, making as much noise as possible just to be mean (I heard you do it a number of times, and I did it, too), the frying pan lurching all around the sink, we made it sound like a big tin bell to wake up the one who was horizontal, spoons falling onto the stainless steel and sounding like a drum, the clink-clink of glasses about to be smashed to smithereens, the chattering of fragile white earthenware dishes that made you want to stamp them into the floor like at a Greek wedding, hold a smashing karaoke like they do in Japan, where they put loud music on for people in a room with vases and old TV sets and they give them a baseball bat so they can break it all apart. Fuck the dining room set, blow up the wedding gifts, the family love, the lists, set the Flox on fire, dynamite the house and be waiting for the newlyweds with a machine gun as they greet everyone in the atrium like a scene from *The Godfather*. And the other one, from bed: "Everything alright, my love?" "Yes, everything's great!" "Did something break?" "No, nothing's broken." What do you want? Tell me want you want. I want war, I thought. I want a guerra against you. But I never said a word.

It must have been past ten. On Plaza Houssay a group of skaters was trying out difficult jumps. They would fail and try again. We had to talk, that was certain. But I didn't expect what you ultimately told me. I also didn't expect, passing by the Hospital de Clínicas, that ten hours later they would be taking me to that emergency room in an ambulance. A few months of debt and the private hospitals shut you out. The operator made that clear when you called. Me with a fever of a 104 degrees, shaking, sitting in a bathtub full of lukewarm water that felt freezing to me. They told you that not only were they not going to send over a doctor, but also that they would not be able to receive me at any clinic. "Your husband has no coverage." So they took me to the public hospital. The horror, our great state nightmare, death guaranteed, and yet, in ten minutes they had plugged me into an IV with who knows what miracle droplets, and I started to recuperate, and they even put me under observation in a room with some other fragile saps. Public hospital. And here I'd been trying to avoid paying import tariffs.

The gigantic Clínicas building greeted me as I passed, said, *See you in a little while,* but I didn't pay it any mind. I was caught up in our fury. I crossed Larrea. Half a block away was the Mix telo, where some time ago I had gone with one of my students at the university. I remember that one time I went to the kiosk next door to buy condoms, it was raining, she appeared. Skirt and laced boots. Smiling. I remember all of her tattoos. We'd see each other there some Fridays before class. Then we would each show up separately. In order not to arouse any suspicion, I would try to dry my hair with the dryer they had screwed into the wall. And her with her hair wet, listening to me from her desk. It must have lasted a couple of months. Then she made up with her boyfriend. She passed the class. She

went to Mexico. I think Maiko was about two. There's a
section of my bandit's tour for you who always want to
know everything.

I turned on Pueyrredón going toward Santa Fe. No
one tried to rob me, no one even saw me. The area was
in terrible shape. Very little light, trash that hadn't been
collected, piles of rotting bags, a few blocks of kiosks with
beat-up signs for ice cream brands. A preview of the Once
neighborhood, without the Orthodox garb. Someone
ought to chronicle Pueyrredón Avenue from the old
French buildings of Recoleta to the peddler heart of the
Recova de Plaza Miserere. The invisible gradation, simply
enumerating, managing to see.

The neighborhood of Villa Crespo, where I'm living
now, is peaceful. Maiko will soon be able to go to the
grocery store to buy things, and a bit after that take the
subway from Corrientes Avenue to your house. Step by
step. It's not time yet. The thing is that the other day he
looked so big to me. We painted the wall of the patio
together, he helped me cook, lit the burner on his own,
chopped tomatoes with an enormous knife. He also helped
me with the pots. I have mint, basil, thyme, rosemary, and
cilantro. I like this place. You never wanted to have plants,
not even on the balcony. I'd like to see your place in
Parque Chas.

I crossed Ecuador, Anchorena, Laprida. There in the
Pelícano telo, I used to meet a Brazilian girl some years
ago. She told me she wanted to translate me. She never

translated a thing. We just fucked, and then she would tell me about the fights she had with her bodybuilding boyfriend and about whether she was going to go back to Belo Horizonte or not. She came and went. She'd fall off the face of the earth for a few months and then show up again suddenly on chat: *Lucas, want to do a Pelican?* Each encounter was an extreme sport. She knew jujitsu, that Brazilian martial art. She'd show me captures and I'd be left unable to breathe, my head pressed between her chocolate thighs. If she'd wanted to, she could have killed me and left me there. Remember how surprised you were at that barbecue when I was playfighting with Nico, and he and I were both drunk, and I subdued him with a capture in the grass? She's the one who taught me that.

I'm not telling you so that you'll tell me. I'm doing it to explain myself to myself. I think that something built up in you. The fact that something was happening in your blind spot filled you with uncertainty. Because I was very careful. I was never with a girl in public. At most it was three meters at the entrance to the telo, where someone could have seen me. That sole moment of risk. The rest was pretty perfectly clandestine. I was extremely careful with the details, I was a good agent. I always came back showered, checked to make sure I didn't have even one long hair attached to me. I deleted every message. But somewhere you knew. Then I calmed down, I took a step back. And then you started up with your late arrivals, your secret agenda, your revenge, conscious or not.

When we came back after that night in the hospital—you too silent, me with the X-rays of my cracked rib in hand—you told me Maiko was going to stay at your mom's place. That was when I saw it coming. "Lucas, what are we going to do? We can't keep going like this. We have to talk to see what we want." You asked me who Guerra was. "Tell me the truth." I told you. You were a bit disillusioned, I felt you wanted something fuller. My little long-distance romance was childish to you. You needed a boost from me to tell me yours. Regardless, you launched in. I never thought you'd say: "I'm in love with someone, she's a friend of mine." "A woman? But you're not a lesbian." "I don't know if I'm a lesbian, but I'm attracted to her," you told me. That she was a doctor, that she worked at Trinity, that you'd met her at a cock-tail hour on a terrace with the foundation, that she had sent you emails and WhatsApp messages, that you'd met up with her, that you'd smoked pot at her place, that you had loved each other for almost a year now, and you weren't going to hide it anymore.

I was kind of catatonic, I remember. It was toward that news that the naïve zombie was going now, down Santa Fe Avenue, among the closed clothing stores. I didn't see it coming, I have to admit. I was sure you were seeing a doctor from the foundation, a guy. I'd have put all my money on that. I hadn't thought it could be a woman. It was just a few more blocks, and I felt I might actually faint. I was cold and hot at the same time. My head was pounding. I guess I'm still processing it and still in pain. Were you not attracted to men anymore, or was it just me? I didn't understand. Your mom asked me over the phone, I didn't know what to tell her, your dad wouldn't talk to you for two months, it was a bombshell among your cousins and our friends. All of them on my side at first; and then they started to understand. And I remained wounded, sexually, I mean, the injured male, depressed. Is that why I'm throwing in your face all the girls I fucked, even though you no longer care? It hurts, but I don't feel hatred, not even anger.

Lately I've been seeing my yoga instructor. Once a week, the morning I don't go into the radio station. She's taught me a lot. Tantric things. She has kids who are grown and don't live with her anymore. She's five years older than I am. Fifty. An honest-to-god MILF. She doesn't want to fall in love, or have kids (she can't anymore), or go to the movies with me. We get together, and we "put all the tinsel on each other's trees," as she puts it. What happens between us is really quite something. I'll spare you the details, but the one thing I do want to tell you about is this moment that tends to repeat. She likes to fuck standing up. She bends over a kind of sideboard, I don't know what it's called, it's a piece of furniture where she has all her family photos, except for her ex-husband they're all there, sons, daughters-in-law, her parents, Russian ancestors, a temporal range of photos from black and white to the first digital ones when we didn't know yet how to take off those red little numbers that gave the date. People smiling on trips, on beaches, in all different landscapes, on top of camels, with dogs, with cats. You get it. My point is that what she's most turned on by is being fucked hard while you grab her by the hips, or the hair, and that slamming motion gradually knocks every one of those photos onto the carpet. That old family altar keeps crashing down, and she can't come until with a single swipe she throws the few frames that remain on the sideboard onto the floor.

I say this because lately I've been thinking a lot about family and marriage. It's going to sound like I think I'm better than everyone, but I'm serious: there has to be another way. We grew up inside this idea of family that wound up filling us with anguish when we saw the cracks in it. All this to say I don't have any problem with Maiko living with you and your partner the days he isn't with me. Secondly, I have no problem meeting her—in fact, I'd like to meet her, I'd like you both to come over if you want for dinner, and I'd like for Maiko to see the three of us, and if I am ever in a real relationship again I'd like it if we could all run into each other without being awkward or anxious. I'd like it if we could do something together, maybe even take a vacation together. If we don't want to rent one house for all of us, then maybe we could at least spend a week at the same beach. Or maybe that's too much, but what I want to say is that Maiko's family is a new thing now. We need to have the courage to throw the photos on the floor. Your decision took a lot of courage.

I guess the idea of family has changed. Now it's kind of like those little interlocking bricks. Everybody puts them together as best they can. The other day I felt like watching *Tremble, Ye Tyrants* on YouTube, I saw old episodes and, among the minute things that happened in one of those weeks in Uruguay, one was a triple wedding between Guerra, César, and Rocío. The image lasts for five seconds. It says something like this: "This week a *Star Wars* convention was held, some kids juggled in Tacuarembó, there was a roller-skating contest, a girl did a handstand on the promenade, Cristóbal the dog couldn't drink his water because he had frost on his dish, the first triple wedding was held in Montevideo . . ." It's a quick image, two pregnant brides in white, and the groom in the middle, all laughing, on a patio, in an alternative ceremony, almost a parody of marriage, invented by them. There was Guerra with her big belly. I had to pause the image to recognize her. Those three had done something right. Afterward I got on Facebook and on her friend's page (since Guerra had deleted hers): there they were, both of them, with their babies in their arms. One of the photos showed César with a spoon in each hand, simultaneously feeding both his kids with their different mothers. Maybe they really lived together, the five of them. I don't know because Guerra and I don't correspond anymore, things quieted down and then fell silent.

I'm glad she had a baby. She looked happy in the video. Even if in the more domestic pictures she looks tired. You might be wondering how I could still be thinking occasionally about a girl who robbed me or got me robbed. But I'm 98 percent certain that it wasn't her. That 2 percent is the silence after the second kick, a glitch in the matrix, a tiny blip in my brain that is never going to go away. I owe Guerra at least the benefit of the doubt, and I let her hover there in my idealized Uruguay, hiding inside of a song that only I know.

It's been a year now, I can get out of my obsession with that day now, and this week I'll finish paying you back the money you loaned me. Thank you for the comfortable installments you let me pay it in. I still owe my brother. Working at the radio isn't really my thing, that's true. I get tired of the witty assholes, those predictable jokes, the amorphous interruptions, and sometimes I deeply desire the apocalypse, a meteorite that wipes us out like it did the dinosaurs. But, besides that, I generally work in peace despite the reprehensible schedule that has me start at six in the morning. Above all, what makes me happy, Cata, is that we have simplified. Not having a car was hard at first, but it's a relief to have gotten free of that huge lump that heated up in the sun, sucked down hectoliters of gas, demanded constant fixing, imported parts, washes, parking, kept me in traffic for hours on end on highways with their asphalt burning. No more car. Putting Maiko in public school was a good move, too. He's adapted well. Sometimes when I go to pick him up, I notice how we progressive parents see each other without saying anything, just glance at each other out of the corner of our eyes, we hear each other's accents of camouflaged snobs. Another thing Maiko rapidly adapted to was spending half the week with me and half with you. Maybe he over-adapts, but the other day a dumbass neighbor asked him, "Did you come to visit your papa?" and he said to her, "I didn't come to visit him, I live with him, too." A magnificent young man. The days I don't see him, I miss him, and I write quite a bit. The book of columns came out in Bogotá. If you want I'll give you a copy, but you already read almost all of them when they were coming out as articles. It's dedicated to you. The Brazilian novel stayed in some neural nebula. But I'm working on a book of poems, and, very slowly, another novel, but no Amazonian adventures, no narcos or gunfights or knives, just a few kicks on the other side of the river. Peripeteia in neighboring states. I'm not going to tell you much because otherwise it'll lose momentum. Once a month I send Enzo a column for his magazine. The guys in Spain from Astillero keep asking for their book. Easy does it.

This is it. My chronicle of that Tuesday is coming to an end. I walked the last block between grunts and moans. What was left of me arrived at the door to the building. The neighbor from the tenth floor was just leaving, the woman who used to go downstairs with her poodle to the consortium meetings. I went in and took the elevator up. In the mirror I was horrifying. That wasn't the same face that had taken the elevator down that morning. Deadly pallor, sunken eyes, disheveled hair, rumpled clothing, out of alignment, asymmetrical, hunched over, filthy, beaten, guilty, and covered in kilometers. And with the instrument for my son in my hand. It had been seventeen hours. The things I had experienced that morning—happiness on the bus, for example—seemed like they had happened in the distant past. It had been a long day. What had yours been like, from the morning when we said goodbye? And Guerra's? And her boyfriend, César's? And Mr. Cuco's? May death be to know all. For now, I can only imagine. If I could narrate the exact day of that dog with all its details, smells, sounds, intuitions, comings and goings, then I would be a great novelist. But that much imagination I do not possess. I write about what happens to me. And what happened was that the elevator reached our floor. I opened the doors, closed them, and rang the bell. In the pause before I heard your voice, I experienced the certainty that I loved you as I continue to love you and as I will always love you, no matter what. It was very late, and from the other side of the door I heard you ask: "Who is it?" I answered: "It's me."

A NOTE ON THE AUTHOR
AND TRANSLATOR

PEDRO MAIRAL is a professor of English literature in Buenos Aires. In 1998 he was awarded the Premio Clarín de Novela and in 2007 he was included in the Hay Festival's Bogotá39 list, which named the thirty-nine best Latin American authors under thirty-nine. Among his novels are *A Night with Sabrina Love*, which was made into a film and widely translated, and *The Woman from Uruguay*, which was a bestseller in Latin America and Spain and has been published in twelve countries.

JENNIFER CROFT was awarded the Man Booker International Prize in 2018 and was a National Book Award Finalist for her translation of Olga Tokarczuk's *Flights*. She is the recipient of Fulbright, PEN, MacDowell, and National Endowment for the Arts grants and fellowships, as well as a Tin House Workshop Scholarship for her memoir *Homesick*. She has published her own work and numerous translations in the *New York Times*, *VICE*, *n+1*, the *New Republic*, the *Guardian*, the *Chicago Tribune*, and elsewhere.